DO WHAT THE BOSS SAYS:

STORIES OF FAMILY AND CHILDHOOD

MICHAEL LOVEDAY

BAMBOO
DART
PRESS

LOS ANGELES † NEW YORK † LONDON † MELBOURNE

Do What the Boss Says by Michael Loveday

978-1-947240-59-9   Paperback
978-1-947240-60-5   eBook

'Anxiety of Influence': "The red god rock / watches all that passes."
from the poem 'Pilgrim', by Eunice de Souza.

Cover art by Dennis Callaci

Layout and design by Mark Givens

For information:

Bamboo Dart Press

chapbooks@bamboodartpress.com

Bamboo Dart Press 027

www.pelekinesis.com

www.bamboodartpress.com

www.shrimperrecords.com

for Lynda and David

Contents

Anxiety of Influence

She was hanging onto the yellow plastic stirrups suspended from the carriage ceiling when the thought struck her: she could do whatever she wanted here. It was nearly midnight. There were no other passengers. An idea wound through her mind: the poem above the window. For the whole journey towards her father's house, as she'd steadied herself to meet him again and watched a ghost version of herself reflected in the glass, its code had been riddling in her subconscious. *The red god rock / watches all that passes.* Words stared down at her as if to admonish. What lesson did they prescribe?

She stepped closer to the window, dared to reach up. Wobbling on her feet, stretching and putting out a hand for balance, she slid the advert precisely to the right, dragged it from position. With a flourish she pulled the cardboard through the air to her side. Revealed behind, in the empty slot, were row upon row of the same icon: a hissing snake, a placeholder print, as if a computer key had got stuck.

The poem slipped under her jumper, wrapping its curve around her belly, the ends almost touching at the small of her back. A shock on her skin, cold and unwelcome as a stethoscope. But—as the corners of the cardboard jutted out from her clothes—she needed this transgression. Middle finger to the system. Or to something.

She paused; the train slowed. The next station took

longer than usual to arrive. Doors opened—a giddy leap to a platform drenched with moonlight. She started the walk to the barrier. Beyond, the dark road twisted away towards her former home.

At the exit gates, a man readied his challenge: russet hair, freckles, bristled beard—the spit of her father, sentry-stiff and evaluating all.

Red god. Rock. She brazened herself, holding his gaze at every step. All she had were words, words, words, the poetry itching within her.

My Double

I made a cardboard cutout of me. Clodagh, I called her, and my family took to her well. That first evening at dinner, they barely registered any difference, as they slurped, and gnawed, and licked their lips, and gorged on lavish meats. At last I didn't have to be disgusted by the sound of them eating. I spent more time alone in my bedroom, reading tales of the headless Dullahan grinning on his night-black horse, and slowly starving myself, praying I would one day become invisible.

My parents grew to like that Clodagh endured, without disruption, their long-and-short-of-it stories of misfortune. And it suited my brother Aidan that Clodagh never ate the food in front of her, so he could sneak spare chips for himself. A cloak of relief settled itself over the house.

Soon it was clear that my family preferred the cardboard me. I let them dress Clodagh in an overcoat and drag her to the park when there was an outing. My Aunt Cath's birthday, Easter Sunday Mass, a bank holiday at Skerries—Clodagh was squeezed into the boot of the car and took my place on all these occasions.

I wouldn't have suffered except Clodagh seemed increasingly perfected, her smile ever more winsome, her clothes pristine, her hair now tidily combed, a smart-arse gleam appearing in her eye instead of the dopey expression my parents always chided me for. I was never this brilliant, never this lovable.

I'd wanted to no longer be part of my family, but I wanted to be missed at the same time.

Baffled, I began to deface my picture-postcard self. Something compelled me to snick at her skin with a Swiss Army knife. I ripped the edges of her fingers where they pointed absurdly at nothing in particular. I graffitied abuse across her forearms. I yearned to rip her goddamn dazzling head off.

Slowly I disfigured Clodagh, until finally my parents could see the path that they'd set their children walking down. Both of us, cutout and I, faced the same ravaged future. We were no more than scrap, ready to be thrown on the fire. Ash amongst ash, we could keep each other company through the long Dublin winter.

Russian Dolls

We were hiding in a broom cupboard under the stairs with our dolls, huddled together and giggling, as sisters do. Ken was humping Barbie, then Barbie was humping Ken. Elysia shone a torch on their salmon-pink bodies. "It's more like *this*," she said, with the superior wisdom of a ten-year old, slapping Ken's groin against Barbie's. "It has to be really hard for Barbie to have a baby."

Will Barbie really have a baby? I thought. Will she have to be taken back to the shop? Is there a special trick, where a child's already inside and someone breaks Barbie open and pulls it out? I'd seen my mother's crimson Russian dolls sitting plump on the window ledge. They hid new versions of themselves inside each other, like someone carrying a secret.

"I kissed Antony on Saturday," Elysia announced. Ken stopped humping Barbie to listen. "A proper kiss," Elysia said. "A grown-up kiss. You know how grown-ups kiss, Georgie?"

"Of course," I said, refusing to sound curious. I took Ken, Barbie and the torch out of Elysia's hands and laid the dolls side by side in a pool of yellow light.

"They touch tongues," Elysia continued. "Antony showed me. It's how you're supposed to do it."

"Ken and Barbie don't use tongues."

"They're toys, der-brain."

"If they were supposed to use tongues then they'd give them tongues, so it's done properly."

"Don't be stupid, Georgie. It's easy. You should learn, so you'll be ready when it's your first turn with a boy. I'll show you."

My sister grasped my shoulders and pushed her tongue between my lips. It wriggled like a wet mouse in my mouth. I let the torch drop out of my hand. She leaned back and the mouse ran away.

"Now you know how to do it," she said, "you won't be nervous next time. Don't tell anyone you practised with me first."

I went back to manipulating Barbie's body and looked down at her immaculate limbs, nodding to myself. In the darkness, I sensed the walls of the cupboard closing in around me. I was one of my mother's Russian Dolls. Some kind of new secret shifted under my skin.

The History of The Child and the Door

The father had to get the child through the door. Mother, sister, cat, rat and hamster had been through the door already. But the boy would not go.

Either the child was unwilling or unable. The father couldn't tell which—there were fine margins involved. He decided the child must be merely unwilling, and that force was the remedy. The father nudged him, but the boy wailed and resisted. The father clamped his hands around the boy's head and tried to shove him towards the door-frame but still he would not budge.

"If you go through this door," said the father, "I will love you with all my heart". But this sounded, even to the father, like a wheedling threat.

"If you go through this door, you will receive a glittering reward," the father then said. But the words were as empty as those discarded hermit crab shells that children pluck from the beach and put to their ears.

Now, the father walked through the door to show the boy how good it was to have done so. "See how much pleasure I got from that," he pleaded, from the other side. "What a sense of accomplishment!" But the child remained fixed where he was, his arms crossed tight together, his sullen mouth knotted and pouting.

The root of the problem had to lie buried in some secret and invisible impossibility. Meanwhile, mother, sister, cat, rat and hamster all watched from the other side of the door. "We love you, child," said those among them who were blessed with the gift of speech, "and we need you to join us." At this the child seemed to hesitate, his defences unsettled. Would he relent at last, they wondered, and walk through?

"I do not like doors," said the boy, finally. "They are like windows, but worse." And he closed the door hard, and locked it, leaving his family bereft on the other side.

(d), (d), (d)

I tell my ninety-two-year-old mother I'm retreating to a small village in the Andalusian mountains. She has Zoom and an iPad, but I will most likely never see her in person again. Does she...

   a) *clap her hands and suggest we open the Tesco prosecco she's been storing since I was born.*
   b) *scream "I forbid it!!!" and throw seven decorative plates on the floor which smash into my bare feet.*
   c) *not listen—she never listens—but continue watching old VHS recordings of The Price is Right from the 1980s (where she would have liked us both to remain, embedded in host Lesley Crowther's arms).*
   d) *none of the above. She is silent. We have both been preparing by leaving each other over and over in our hearts for decades.*

Despite my disappointment, when I say goodbye, I kiss her warmly on the cheek. Does she...

   a) *recoil from my kiss and pat me on the head. "There, there," she says, "you'll get over me soon, Tarquin. I'll become only a distant, painless memory." Tarquin was my father's name.*
   b) *grab both sides of my face and upgrade my polite cheek-brushing into a full-blown lip-smacker. "There's more*

where that came from, Tarquin," she says, winking. Tarquin was my closest friend at school.

c) *say, "Ah, I remember when you used to hug me so hard every day it would nearly put my back out. I wish you'd never aged past seven. Oh look," she adds, "Tarquin's been at the bins again." Tarquin is the irrepressible local squirrel.*

d) *none of the above. We are both too devastated to talk.*

As I drive away, failing my mother again, and seeing her for what may be the last time, does she...

a) *text me before my car's out of sight, saying "Don't forget to call when you arrive. Allow me this silliness. We never stop worrying."*

b) *run up the driveway, smashing her hands on the boot of my Hyundai. "When did you last wash this junk-heap? You're no son of mine!" Her own Audi gleams even though it hasn't been driven for ten years.*

c) *stand in the doorway, waving sentimentally until she thinks I can no longer see her, then letting her expression fall and shaking her head in some form of deep-rooted intergenerational disapproval.*

d) *write me this story on a postcard, leaving the twelve multiple choice options blank, then post it to Andalusia, asking me to complete and return it. We smuggle tiny glimpses of our half-lived lives.*

When she came to me one morning, all wet-eyed and incoherent, you'll forgive my surprise:

"I've done it, Lulu," she said. "It's over."

"What's over, mum?"

Her hands were fidgety. She was chewing her lower lip. "Kevin. I showed him alright."

"Who's Kevin?"

"Kevin, that guy I've been telling you about for the last six years." I had no idea who Kevin was. "The guy who's been screwing me up all this time. Now who's screwed up!"

Over and over my mum had rescued me from my crises when I'd no right to expect help. Debts, dictator-boyfriends, reckless colleagues—mum would materialise, rescuing her daughter with a miracle cheque, a hug, a re-written email. Mum was always right about my world.

"Mum, what have you done?"

"I left a letter for his wife. At their home. He's away in Oslo—some... conference." She voiced the word with disdain. "By the time he gets back he'll be ruined." She picked at a flap of skin at the corner of her mouth then swallowed it.

When you've watched someone graduate from shit-soiled nappies to shit-ridden adulthood, you're entitled to act the authority. But now her face was so pale it made me uncomfortable.

"Well, whoever he is and whatever you've done, he deserves it," I said. "You've always told me not to lead a double life."

They'd been lovers, she confessed, since my dad died. He'd promised to take care of her, leave his marriage, fill *the hole in her days*. And now, after six years, my mum had klaxxonned her existence to Kevin's silicone-enhanced wife.

I turned down the brawl of the TV—some European circus act cavorting round the inside of a tent—and sat on the rented sofa beside her, reaching my arm over her shoulder. "Mum, it's okay. The world's not ending. You're safe, you're loved."

Except she seemed inconsolable. The regret was evident in broken, sobbed phrases, her reluctance to drag her gaze from the floor. Maybe she should've given him a bit more time. She'd risked the whole relationship. He'd never forgive.

I'd heard her say it to me a hundred times: *you are safe, you are loved*. Now I realised you could speak the words without really believing them.

"You've stood up for yourself," I said. "He was stringing you along. Like biker Dave did to me, remember? What did you tell me then?"

"I don't remember," she said. In front of me, a blonde in a

Tarzan suit clung to a trapeze. The audience laughed and clapped.

"You said—he doesn't deserve you. When you finally act like people have to earn your love, the right one will come along."

"I said that?"

"Yes." She seemed surprised, as if it hadn't been her truth. She ran a hand over the arm of the sofa. A layer of dust lifted into the light. I couldn't remember exactly what she'd said either.

"Love yourself more than you love another. Remember? I still have that letter you wrote me. *Stand up and fight for your life.*"

She looked at me, confused, then stared back at the TV, eyes glazing over. I went on, inventing a chain of quotations. At last I knew that something hidden within me was alone, unreachable, and always had been—and within everyone else too, for that matter. It felt solid and safe and cold—a slab lodged in the tender muscle of every heart.

The Tarzan blonde hung upside-down, dangling on the backs of her knees. My mother and I watched a ring of men approach from below and hurl blazing torches at her outstretched hands.

Once upon a time there was a couple who wanted a child. The woman was a portrait painter, but portraits were out of fashion. Her husband was a clay worker; he too had only ever made a meagre living. They longed for a child to alleviate their woes, but none appeared.

One day, though, later in her life than they had thought possible, the woman discovered she was pregnant. She gave birth to a beautiful girl. And the girl's heart was made of silver.

"It can't be true!" her parents said.

"Silver as a coin," said the doctor, holding up shocked X-rays.

The parents rejoiced: this child must be special indeed.

The girl rarely cried out of hunger and she did as she was told. She manifested no tantrums, shed no tears and quickly attuned to her parents' moods and whims. As she grew up, when her parents were whining about their careers, acquaintances or clothes, she listened generously with an adult's compassion. She was altogether a remarkable creature.

One day, after the husband had completed his accounts in a hard, hard year, he said to his wife:

"What if we took a little silver from her heart, and sold it to buy some better clothes? It would be such a small sliver of silver she would barely notice."

His wife reluctantly agreed. So they cut open their daughter's chest while she slept and extracted a slice of her silver heart and sewed her back up again. The girl bled for a month until the stitches healed. But she did not complain and she told no one.

Her parents bought the clothes and they bought their daughter some clothes too—the silver was so fine and pure that they could easily afford it. And they felt grateful.

Another year passed, harder than the last. The wife said:

"If only we could enjoy some fine dining with our friends this year to make up for our struggles." She hesitated; then she went on. "What if we cut out another sliver of silver from our daughter's heart? I suppose she would not miss it?"

The husband conceded this was true. So they sliced out some more silver. And the daughter bled for a month and this time was in pain. Yet she said nothing and instead painted landscapes with the blood seeping from her chest. Her landscapes were even finer than her mother's portraits, and the girl was comforted that her wound proved useful. Her mother asked her: "Where did you find paint of such rich colour?" The girl answered that she had used the blood-red earth straight from their back yard. The mother was secretly irked that her daughter's paintings were more beautiful than her own; but she harboured little grievance because she was now richer in more tangible ways. The parents enjoyed sumptuous meals with their peers. They bought themselves jewellery apt for such occasions. And they gave their daughter canvases, in order to indulge her new hobby as good parents should.

Another hard year, another opening of the daughter's body, another extraction. A new home this time, closer to a more opulent district. And more bleeding, and more paintings made from the matter that wept from the child. And thus it continued, year after year: she carried less and less silver in her heart and painted more and more beautiful landscapes. Her parents lived richly on the proceeds of her heart.

Soon, the parents were old before their time, and very little of the child's silver remained. Her paintings were coveted through the land, though she had never wanted to sell them. And her parents had grown fat on their unaccustomed wealth.

Then the husband and wife took one last piece of silver from their daughter's body—and bought golden goblets and vintage wines, and held an extravagant party to charm their friends. They looked forward to a lifestyle even more splendid than before.

The next morning, though, they both collapsed and died. Their daughter must arrive at adulthood as an orphan.

From the moment of her parents' death, she bled no

more. She could make no more paintings when she had no blood to give. She must sell the landscapes even though she'd insisted that she never would. She knew no other way to survive.

She held a private view on the evening of her parents' funeral, inviting all the well-to-do folk who had known her parents in the wealthier years of their life. She sold all her paintings, and their renown grew when she confessed the manner of their making. Blood landscapes were just the thing.

Through the exhibition she had earned a small fortune, enough to live for the rest of her days in a manner even finer than that of her parents.

But she could not enjoy a single day of her life thereafter, for her heart was now empty.

Push/Pull

Towelling myself down, I emerge from the shower in my father's house, a few days after the funeral. I've been sifting dusty memories into bin bags and suitcases, deciding what to keep.

Once I'm dry, I pull at the door back to the bedroom. It snags—the top of the door is caught on the lintel. I pull harder, remembering this problem from childhood. Every few months, the door always shifted, some ghost in the hinges leaving it stuck. My father used to shave more and more millimetres off the top edge, adjust the hinges, and more and more light would creak in at the base where the door, over the years, was repelling itself from the floor.

The door, this time, won't budge. When I tug at the handle, it bangs loose at the base but the upper part remains lodged into the frame. I wrench downwards. No joy.

"Pull harder," a voice tells me.

I yank the handle harder.

"Puny little kid," comes the voice from beyond the door.

Enough! I've got this. I stand on a chair and try to prise the top of the door away with my fingertips. There's nowhere to grip.

"You'll never get out, you filthy child! Ha-ha!!!"

I imagine the speaker so pleased with himself, pressing

both hands together, aiming them at me, then kissing the smoking barrel with joy.

With that, the bulb in the bathroom blows and the room goes dark. A thin strip of light gleams under the door.

Climb out of the window? It's a straight two-storey drop. Throw the chair at the door? The door is more solid than the chair. Wait for someone to release me? But who? My phone is on the other side of the door. All my belongings, and all my father's belongings, are on the other side of the door.

"You've only got yourself to blame," cackles the voice.

I get down on my knees and squint below the door. Someone's eye greets me.

"Open this damn door!" I holler.

"What did I warn you?" A hiss like a viper's breath, through the crack at the base.

The door refuses to budge, as stuck as it ever was.

My body is starting to feel cold.

"Not so clever now, boy?"

Let me be. Let me be. Let me be.

"The problem with you," says his mother, "is that you love failure."

Neil doesn't hear the words at first, just keeps scribbling around the cryptic crossword. *For stimulation, no English client is taking an alternative (8).* Like his mother, it's been nagging at him all morning.

"You sit there in your dressing gown. It's one o'clock and you haven't shaved or showered. I'm not sure you've had breakfast. And I won't even ask whether you've cleaned your teeth."

He doodles letters in a gap on the newspaper. He's sure this one's an anagram. Glitch...?? Gnash...?? The words he glimpses can't be right.

"Poring over every single column in the paper, slouched before the TV all afternoon—why don't you get up and paint something?"

"Will you shush for two minutes, Mother? I'm trying to think. This is a tricky one."

"Brush, canvas, paint. It's not that tricky."

"I'm having an intentional fallow season. To feed my creative spirit."

"If you really want to feed yourself, then put a shift in and earn some money. Painters, they go out into those meadows and find *stuff* to look at. Or if not landscapes, then

24

portraits. Life! It's already out there! What's fallow about that?"

Maybe it's not an anagram, he wonders.

"I'm getting tired of watching you mope about. It's not healthy in a man of your age. Honestly, you get out of bed but it's as if you're fast *asleep*. Or on drugs. Which you probably are, come to think of it. And if you're not going to paint, isn't it about time you hunted down a proper job? Or a relationship? You can't stay here scrounging off me forever, what kind of a life is that?!"

"Clitoris!" he cries, then puts his pen down.

The Glass House

Glass ceiling, yes, but also glass walls, glass doors. Glass bed. Glass pillow. Most of me lived there, in the glass house, but I like to think I kept a part of me living in a dream home made of brick and wood and soft, plush sofas, an elsewhere to which I could one day move.

Through the glass, my mother could monitor all aspects of my life. She would sneak glances while she inspected the garden fence or ripped unwelcome weeds from the soil. In my father's absence, we forged a long-term contract: fettered but secure.

One night, while my mother slumbered indoors in the main house, I stayed awake and buried secrets in the turf that made up the floor beneath me—daughterly opinions, scraps of shameful fictions I'd been scrawling about the house and all its tempers—things that had proved impossible to shelter safely within a house of glass. I dug holes with my hands, hid the secret things and covered them over with earth. I fell asleep, exhausted. I had buried so many that when I woke, I forgot which lay hidden where, at what depth, and for what purpose. But the buried things still seemed to be present, like the feeling of a pair of spectacles after it has been removed from the head.

I thought: now my mother knows nothing of my real truth. I couldn't help but weep a little. But then, from the damp soil at my feet, wild nettles and elegant roses unfurled themselves.

It was impossible to distinguish which were good and which were bad. I was afraid my mother would see them. I was tempted to tug them out of the ground—but for the prickles and thorns.

And then I understood why my mother could not let me leave.

The nettles and roses grew. They crowded—thick, fast, triumphant—against the glass roof and walls.

i.

What do I do when my father tells me to buy a can of striped paint? I set out keenly, of course; this is my first day, my first job, in a summer of quests and adventures. *Do what the boss says.* If factory workers don't follow instructions, all manner of cogs could fall off the grand machine.

The store owner sees me coming from ten miles off. "Striped paint? We sold the last tin of green and yellow at eleven. Popular stuff. Run along to Carson & Co., they may have some."

Same tale from Carson & Co. Return to the factory, downcast. My father tuts.

ii.

What do I do when he's ravenous for a ham salad doughnut? I go eagerly, of course; I'm a good boy, he's famished, I comply with my father's request. If children don't learn to do what fathers say, all manner of doors shall be closed.

Café after café is out of stock. A sudden run on ham salad doughnuts today. They do taste so, so good. Try Bryce's place.

Try Perry's. Try Campbell's. Return to the factory, empty hands, solemn heart. My father shakes his head, slowly.

iii.

What do I do when he needs a long weight, the heaviest kind? I go earnestly, of course; third errand in a week and I've fluffed the first two. If paupers won't learn to dig up the treasure, all manner of riches will remain hoarded and obscure.

I reach the hardware shop, certain of victory. The cashier heads off out back. I wait.

And wait. And wait.

The Memory of Flesh

Thumbs have a longer memory than some other parts of the body: there are times when the body doesn't forget. Click down, click up. A small circle left on the flesh. By this mark, the power-that-must-be measures the quality of my attention. If, by the time the Cathedral closes, a deep ring shows there, He will deem my day worthwhile.

I no longer notice the colour of these visitors' hair, whether they have green eyes or an angular nose, whether they wear washed-out jeans or a balaclava. It's just a slow horde passing: a secular congregation. I fulfil the basics of their questions: "Where are the toilets?", "Parlez-vous Français?" We talk, but never talk.

They never ask me how I am, what I long for, or what still keeps me up at night. I might as well myself be a relic.

Long ago, my father used to preach that everyone in God's garden merited attention. I paid attention. As a child, I would sit in the back of his burgundy Honda and clench my teeth gently every time we passed by someone we knew, a neighbour who might care. Not quite exactly on time: just behind the beat, like a jazz singer.

It was a ten-minute walk from Harrow-on-the-Hill station to the cinema, and I set off with a cocksure bounce in my stride. Seeing *Hellraiser* would be the climax to a good week. Things seemed finally to be falling into shape at school after a bad year since Dad died. I'd spent three terms feeling like my skin had been unpeeled. But this week, out of nowhere, Bryony had written to me, sounding like she wanted me back. I'd made it into the 1st XV. And I'd been offered a place at my second choice uni, after nothing but bluffing at interview. I was sick of near-misses. Maybe I was seeing some luck.

It was seven o'clock and dark. Buses were funnelling down Station Road. The pavements were quiet; most of the shops were already closed. I hadn't put on enough layers and the late October chill cut through me. I pulled my duffle hood over my head, plunged hands into pockets, and kept walking the walk.

I was rounding the junction with Sheepcote Road, when a couple came striding arm in arm towards me. They wore matching blue jeans and black Puffa jackets. His hair was shaved close to his scalp. She was much taller than him, like he'd have to stand on something just to kiss her. They seemed older—in their late twenties. She laughed and tipped back her head to puff out cigarette smoke. The guy curled a fat arm like a slug round her shoulders. I felt a trapdoor drop open inside me.

Then, before they'd passed, the guy said:

"You looking at my girlfriend?"

I stopped. "No. Of course not."

"You saying she's not fit then?"

"What?"

"You're not looking at her. So she's not fit?"

"No. I mean, I just wasn't looking, that's all."

He stepped closer. "Yeah?" He grinned at me, teeth glinting in the dark. "And what if I had a knife?"

Closer again. My heart—thudding. I couldn't see his hands well enough to judge. His girlfriend stopped laughing. "Jim." She tugged at his arm. "Leave the boy alone."

"What if I had a knife," he said again, "and I stabbed you in the ribs?"

He stood right up next to me. I could smell the beer on his breath. I knew what might be next. The weird thing was, I didn't move away. Maybe he would kill a little part of me. His hand was clenched in his pocket, and then it was coming for me—and I just waited for it.

The World's Best Daughter

Ten thousand doors, opening and closing in succession—and through those doors, ten thousand worlds I must abandon as I greet them. I screw my mind into the task. My hand is callused, ankles weak, calves cramped and burning.

Father readies his whistle, looks at his watch. A pause for prayer, offered to that God who oversees our cause: He has the power to break the thread of our pulse at any moment of His choosing. Then, one shrill blast and I begin.

I grasp the handle, push until the black door gives, step through, then close the door behind. *Turn!* my father cries. I face the same door's white reverse, drag it open, cross and stand exactly where I stood before. *Turn!* he cries, again.

Over the fence, our neighbour watches: "Fools." He spits and walks away.

My father built this door soon after I was born. Painted one side black, one white. In a clearing in our small orchard, he fixed its frame into the dirt. *Let no wind rip it down, however wild.* And now, each dawn, I rise and go into the garden. *You'll be the bloom upon our nation's soil.* My father calls from where he waits amongst the trees.

The door has taught me its moods. I am a dancer in a ballet. And at the ceremony's heart, an older emptiness. Our tale is one of earth-poor farmers, reaching hard into the past. *Dream your giant dreams tonight, my love! Soon, you'll free the shackles our family has worn for many years.*

My calling is to learn about the door, its creaks, its swings, its whims of mild resistance. At night, I pick the splinters from my hands until my body plummets into darkness.

I am the fittest of the village children now. Black-white, black-white, repeat—I'll cross more thresholds than anyone before me! Glory will surely come, father says, once the world hears of my feats. Our nation's leader—blessed President! God's envoy!—has offered a great reward.

Little Spider Feet

Miss Dushenka bothered him twice over. First, her nose-picking. It was one thing to have a little rummage occasionally. It was another to be engaged in some extensive archaeological dig and then to eat the remains. All this as she, in motherly fashion, monitored the boys queuing for lunch. It had put him off his sausage and chips. Surely as headmistress she should be a model of good behaviour.

She was a large woman, and she must have been born big. Her mum had neglected her, the boys reckoned, and the result was unstoppable hunger. The nose-picking was just part of her greed for the universe. Even these dirty bits from her body she couldn't resist—she had to find them and cram them into her mouth like she was devouring the last piece of apple pie.

But nose-picking, he decided, watching her carefully as he waited in the first aid room, was only the first problem with the headmistress.

He sat down in the lone wooden chair. Her sweat-sickly aroma filled the small room. She took her place behind him and he tried not to gag at the closeness of her body odour.

"Head still now, Sebastian."

Her hands moved into his crewcut and crawled over his scalp. Her fingers caressed him like the movements of little spider feet.

His neck prickled. The fine, boyish hairs on his forearms alerted themselves. Her chunky fingers kept threading through his brown hair. He shivered as a million tiny electric shocks surged up and down his neck.

The intensity of it! A sheer, weird thrill that stilled him. No matter that she performed this same ceremony for the entire school, a routine check they all had to undergo. This was his and Miss Dushenka's illicit moment.

Inside him, an ache was awakening. Some force was at work that he didn't understand. How he felt was no longer affected by attraction or dislike. His longing was ready to unleash itself at a moment's invitation. It was inevitable, even if it was disgusting and despicable.

And Miss Dushenka *did* disgust him.

This woman that all the boys mocked—even hated. This woman who was simply too gross for the world. He waited, now, for a stray movement, a touch on his body where it didn't belong. He would have consented, in this moment, to anything.

But no such moment came. He felt his face redden as her hands retreated.

"Call the next boy in as you go," she said.

He rose and opened the door.

Parker sat outside, the tip of his too-long nose obscured by the cover of a science textbook.

"Your turn," he said to Parker.

Parker squinted and fiddled with his thick-rimmed glasses.

"How was it?" he said.

"Beastly," Sebastian replied, yet he couldn't bear to walk away.

Halfway Down the Stairs

I wanted to listen to them. To hear how they talked when I wasn't there. Like they were goblins and I was hiding behind trees to study them. Like if I listened, I could feel grown-up too.

They were in the kitchen. I could see their bodies but not their heads—I was above them, halfway up the stairs. I wedged my face through the wooden gaps, imagining what would happen if I got stuck. My step-dad had painted the stairs green last week. They still smelt funny.

"Not yet," Mummy was saying, quietly. "We should wait until Martha finishes school."

Even though they were saying my sister's name, I knew they were actually talking about me. And I knew they were talking about bad things because I'd seen Mummy smash a zillion plates on the kitchen tiles earlier. That's when I'd gone upstairs to play Lego. I'd been making a fort and filling it with animals all week and it still wasn't ready. Martha teases me but I like building things.

Mummy and my step-dad were wearing shoes. But Mummy once said she'd kill me if I brought dirt from my shoes into the kitchen again. And their voices sounded different. Like a few years ago, my step-dad gave me a book that was too hard for me, where the words were too old.

I couldn't hear—someone not yet something.

Martha came out of her bedroom by the top of the stairs and called my name.

"Shall we go out in the garden?"

I shook my head, put my finger to my lips and waved her to sit down. She scrunched up her face and sat on the stairs above me. Then she moved closer, put her hand around mine and we kept quiet. We listened to Mummy and my step-dad. It was like something else was speaking through their mouths. We listened like the words were coming from the future.

Snuffed Candles

Samantha feared, in guilty moments, that she loved the lakes more than she loved her father. Today, on their usual monthly circuit, he hobbled slowly, clutching his stick, and she looped her arm through his. Over the water, boats tacked in the breeze. The lakes looked grimy: Rickmansworth in February wasn't known for its hospitality. Still, she loved strolling through the canalside fields, or drinking in the views of Stockers Lake, where clumps of trees sprouted wildly from the water and geese squabbled on the pontoons.

A walk with her father ought to feel like a noble pursuit, the slice of walnut cake a deserved reward. But they were drowning, as he picked cake crumbs from his teeth, in an account of his last hospital visit. She already knew its disappointments—she'd been there, sobbing alongside him. She didn't want to think about what lay ahead.

She played truant from his tale, caught up in thoughts of Monday's return to a landscape of filing cabinets. Here she was, holed up in the Home Counties, keeping watch on her ex-novelist father as the years performed their slow erosion, her mother long gone, and her own ambitions to be a big nose lawyer in London fizzled out like snuffed candles. Was the sacrifice worth it? Had she repaid her daughterly debts?

She swam to the surface—her father had somehow found

an ending to his story and his cake. He wanted a second circuit of the water. She helped him from his chair and accompanied him back to the first lake, sheltering them both with an umbrella as they walked. Gaunt trees huddled beside the shoreline. Swans honked at a child hurling small chunks of cheese.

A thunderstorm loomed in the distance. Most of the sailboats had packed up now, hunkering down as the rain intensified.

"Look!" Her father pointed at a grey heron by the riverbank. It picked its feet slowly over the grass. "It's an old man from a black and white movie."

She laughed. He seemed pleased. "It's a tailcoated barrister," he added.

"Go on."

"He's nearing retirement. The days run slower now. But he feels no pity for himself."

The heron lifted from the bank. After a few sluggish flaps of its wings, it climbed, easy and elegant and effortless. She closed her eyes, blessed the grace of the bird's wings as it glided through the downpour, blessed the curiosity in her father's words. She willed the moment to stretch out its silence a little longer. The heron would linger for a minute, then soon, like so much else, would be gone.

Every Time We Fall

I lie on the bed with my mother, propped up against the headboard. It's ok. I'm forty-seven but I'm mothering her a little. Broken pelvis, broken shoulder (two falls, one on Christmas morning), she is bed-ridden. I'm stroking her arm. She keeps fidgeting—I don't think she likes it—but I like it. So there.

We're watching TV together here because where else. My father is in the lounge. He is *putting his bloody feet up*, now that I'm here. In the bedroom, we're held by a Netflix programme about people who rescue pets. Wild or tamed, we all need to be rescued; TV is my mother's god. My mother and father have rescued me more often than I can remember, every time I have fallen. But now, Mum wants to slump here with the subtitles on—the only way she comes close to following the story. She wants to ignore the physio's exercises, because they hurt. She wants to not care about eating chocolate as a main meal. And she doesn't want to be nagged.

She already knows the truth of the matter. We all do.

And into this soap opera come the TV dogs being rescued. One has a tumour the size of an orange on its jaw. One can't walk for its matted, tangled, neglected fur. One has misshapen knee bones. Operations, anaesthetic, treatment plans are required. The RSPCA and the veterinary surgeons arrive like war zone relief workers. They perform daily miracles, get their hearts splintered repeatedly by creatures that are beyond remedy.

My mother is crying. She would like all the dogs to be saved. But not her. Parents don't want to be rescued by their children—it hurts, it breaks their bones. They want to be loved. I am learning this much.

TV sounds wash over us.

Acknowledgments

Thanks to the following people who commented on stories from this manuscript: Vanessa Gebbie, Nancy Stohlman, Charmaine Wilkerson, and Will Eaves. And thanks to the following people for help with selections and sequencing: Victoria Collier, Graham Hodge, David Loveday, John Mackay, Damhnait Monaghan, Alison Powell, Maggie Sawkins, Robin Thomas, and Helen Turnbull. Special thanks to my wife Lynda for encouragement and support.

Thanks to the editors of the following journals, where early versions of these stories were published:

Connotation Press: 'Trapeze with Fire-Jugglers'

Fiction Kitchen Berlin: '(d), (d), (d)'

Fictive Dream: 'Silver and Blood'

Flash Fiction Festival Anthology 2022: 'Halfway Down the Stairs'

KYSO Flash: 'Near-Misses', published as 'Knife'; 'The Memory of Flesh', published as 'Click'

National Flash Fiction Day Anthology 2019 ('And We Pass Through'): 'The History of the Child and the Door'

New Flash Fiction Review: 'Snuffed Candles'

Retreat West 10th Anniversary Anthology ('Ten Ways the Animals Will Save Us'): 'The World's Best Daughter'

Snakeskin: 'Anxiety of Influence', published as 'Poems on the Underground'

Sonder: 'Russian Dolls'

The Journal of Radical Wonder: 'Every Time We Fall', 'The Glass House', 'This Be the Curse'

Writing in Education: 'Fallow Season'

X-RAY Lit: 'My Double'

'Little Spider Feet' was shortlisted in the Writers Retreat UK 2020 competition

'Push/Pull' was longlisted in the Retreat West 'Uncanny' Flash Fiction Competition, 2021.

About the Author

Michael Loveday is a fiction writer and poet, and has been an editor and tutor of creative writing for more than a decade. His other publications are: the craft guide *Unlocking the Novella-in-Flash: from Blank Page to Finished Manuscript* (Ad Hoc Fiction, 2022); the hybrid novella-in-flash *Three Men on the Edge* (V. Press, 2018); and the poetry chapbook *He Said / She Said* (Happen*Stance* Press, 2011). Michael lives in Bath, England, and mentors novella-in-flash writers through his online programme at www.novella-in-flash. com.

BAMBOO DART PRESS

112 N. Harvard Ave. #65
Claremont, CA 91711

chapbooks@bamboodartpress.com
www.bamboodartpress.com

INVISIBLE

A DIARY OF ROUGH
SLEEPING IN BRITAIN

ANDREW FRASER

—

With contributions from

FREEDOM ANARCHIST NEWS
CORPORATE WATCH
S.L.A.P.
GEORGE F
and TONY MARTIN

Edited by ROB RAY

INVISIBLE: A DIARY OF
ROUGH SLEEPING IN BRITAIN

Foreword	vii
Introduction	ix
April 2017	1
May	7
June	13
July	29
August	49
September	79
October	93
November	117
December	125
January 2018	145
February	151
March	159
Afterword	165
Notes	193

This first edition published by Freedom Press, 2018

84b Whitechapel High St, London, E1 7QX
freedompress.org.uk

ISBN 978-1-904491-31-6
All rights reserved

Designed by
Euan Monaghan

Cover photograph
by Filip Patock

Printed in the UK
by Imprint Digital

This book is dedicated to Lola's Homeless.

FOREWORD

AIN'T NOTHING GOING ON
BUT THE CLASS WAR ...

The following is a fierce and fresh update from the rebellious streets of the UK, driven along by the sensitively furious diary of Andrew Fraser, and amplified by reports from the autonomous housing struggle currently aflame from Manchester to Bournemouth. Nothing less than the latest chapter in a saga dating back to the very origins of the power struggle between the forces of domination and liberation, personalised and contemporised to our time teetering on the edge of Brexit.

A few years back I wrote a book about squatting in London, and how changes in the law had made it even more precarious for people who would self-house, forcing more and more to live on the streets rather than face imprisonment for occupying one of the many, many empty residential properties in the UK, or regular eviction for making use of a commercial one. Over the ten years since austerity began, the number on the streets have gone up, the number of squatters has gone down, but the number of empty properties has stayed the same. Too fucking many.

Fraser's words sing with a feral howl of frustration and hope, indignation and rage, yet it is as if you had run into Andrew in a pub and were chatting to him over a pint and a packet of crisps. These words are an incitement to take those emotions out into the streets, to seize the opportunity that presents that itself daily: do we continue to dehumanise, to defer, to defend and to destroy? Or do we choose to challenge the logic of submission, and to reach out and seize the possibility of change? No begging pun intended.

Yeah, the following pages drip with the pain and possibilities of freedom and failure, a sketching of a life self-defined within capitalism's prison. A defiant shout in the darkness saying: You Don't Have To F*ck People Over To Survive.

They are soaked with the struggle of centuries of the oppressed against power, of the rich against autonomy, saturated with the needless and anonymous suffering of thousands, anointed with the agony of broken families. They reek of fearlessness and terror, of piss-soaked streets and champagne charity balls, sterile air-con offices and the perfume-stank of crack alleys.

To paraphrase a popular educator of the oppressed named Augusto Boal, the following diary charts a world where there are two ideologies in conflict with one another.

One, the belief that we are all brothers and sisters and others, that we can co-exist in mutual aid and solidarity, that we are all equal and deserving of respect, support, love, generosity, of the qualities of humanity and humanisation. An ideology that says if we are to fall, others are beholden to pick us back up, and brush us off, and the same for us to do for them.

And the other is best explained by the tale of the Raft of Medusa, or in these austere times, the Raft of May-dusa. A true story of a raft of 152 survivors cast adrift by the incompetence and callousness of the aristocratic admiralty that had crashed their ship into the rocks, then abandoned them to their fate on the seas. This raft of 152 men, women and children was lost at sea for 13 days. Within that time, those aboard turned upon one another, driven beyond morality by their desperation. They turned upon the sick, the weak, the defenceless, casting the disabled and elderly into the waters, turning in that short time to cannibalism and barbarism in order to survive, the strong destroying the weak.

— George F

INTRODUCTION

I've been told never start a book with statistics, particularly anything with dates. It ages badly and starts the journey on a flat note. But to begin this story it is important to offer context. *Invisible* covers a year from the Spring of 2017 through to April 2018, told through a combination of the diary of Andrew Fraser, a successful journalist who found himself homeless in 2016/17, alongside accounts and reports of squatters' self-organisation, as well as investigative reporting. It's a human story about struggling in 21st century Britain, told within a broader framework of systemic immiseration of working class people and resistance to that injustice.

In the year this book comes out, the government has pledged to "end rough sleeping" in Britain by 2027. Their method of doing so involves a Parliamentary Act requiring stretched councils to take on specific responsibilities and temporarily bunging £100 million towards help "accessing services" and "with mental health and addiction". Which is a sick joke to anyone who has much experience of Britain's eviscerated public services.

"Ending rough sleeping" is utterly meaningless. In nine years' time no-one will be picking up on that broken vow, in the same way no-one remembers that Boris Johnson promised in 2009 to end rough sleeping in London by 2012, and no-one will harp on about Manchester Mayor Andy Burnham's similar pledge last year to end rough sleeping there by 2020.

Infamously, the last time a serving government made such a pledge was in 1999, when Tony Blair promised to reduce homelessness by two thirds within four years. They proudly announced success in 2001, only for a number of whistle-blowing shop floor workers to report that homeless people had simply been rounded up out of the way on the day when the official survey was held.

This was only a particularly blatant expression of the sort of performance politics which has gone on for time immemorial. Governments make big promises and when they can't deliver, fudge or redefine until it looks like they have. Meanwhile the actual number of people on the street, the people holding out coffee cups for change living in cracks in the wall, does not fall by two thirds. In fact even on the shaky numbers the government puts out, they barely budged through the New Labour years. In 1998 the "official" snapshot count of rough sleepers on a given night in Britain was around 1,800. In 2010 the housing ministry counted … about 1,800.

In 2017's "austerity Britain" (a euphemism for "bury the poor" if ever there was one) however that number climbed to at least 4,751, about a quarter of them in London. I say "at least" because these are snapshots of whoever could be found by researchers on the day. Rough sleepers have been repeatedly driven out of town centres in recent decades however, so the real number is likely to be far higher — homelessness charity Crisis, for example, estimates about 8,000. And that is merely the tip of the real lived experience of having no safe home, as the population of people in temporary accommodation, the "statutorily housed" in suit-speak, has climbed to 300,000. In future years, as councils continue to be starved of resources, it is hard to see how at least some of those won't shift further in their government bracket.

Such raw numbers are changeable, but the lesson is timeless. Governments cannot "eliminate" rough sleeping. They cannot "sort out" homelessness. We can, with enough effort and a fair economic wind, push the State to provide some semblance of a safety net but the bones of the issue are beyond the powers of Ministers and MPs. Their existence is bound up in defending capitalism, an ideology which must have its losers, and their clunking institutions are simply not capable of fixing everything that needs fixing.

Homelessness is often portrayed as a problem to be solved. It is not a "problem" however inasmuch as it is an inevitable part of the economic system we inhabit — evidence of profit and exploited labour working as advertised. If there is a problem to be found, it is in the insistence of the owners that they are not responsible for the creation and reproduction of poverty. When loos are closed to the poor, shit on the streets is framed as a moral failing of the poor. When people being paid a casualised, precarious minimum wage are unable to afford inflated rents, they get slurred as a burden on the State. When the drive to automation strips a million roles from the economy our wise and powerful shareholders, sitting on increased margins, castigate the people they ceased paying as workshy bums.

Our leaders are well aware of this problem even if they won't admit it. In lieu of ever being able to eliminate poverty they simply redefine the concept. A great deal of effort has been made to slice away at the number of people who qualify as the "deserving poor" and the "destitute" so that fewer resources need to be thrown at the problem. The State palms off responsibility to charities and the public wherever possible, notably framed a decade ago by former Prime Minister David Cameron's wretched "Big Society" ploy. But governments being what they are, no-one wants to lose control of the narrative. So we find ourselves in a situation where charities, supposedly independent, are contracted to provide support to homeless people on the proviso that they stop criticising the government whose failings they are patching over. Caught up in a cycle of "competitive tendering," large third sector groups find themselves badmouthing self-organised homeless people [FN// See March 14th, 2018], grasping for spare change that would otherwise go in the coffee cups and quietly working with the government to crack down on homeless migrants [FN// See April 8th, 2017].

But government writ is merely the backdrop. Down among the grassroots are homeless people helping each other, banding together against destitution, helped by small under-funded and selfless groups such as Lola's Homeless. Squatting, long demonised and now legally pressured by the right, remains as a direct action rebuke to the "helpless to solve social problems" rich who leave their multiple properties empty, protect-ed by law and hired guards.

Our intent with this book is to explore two facets of the crisis that has hit Britain, the experiences of rough sleeping and homeless autonomy. We are lucky to have Andrew Fraser's voice in articulating this first aim. He is not a youthful reporter attempting to make a name in gonzo jour-nalism by "surviving" for a couple of weeks. He has lived, and still lives, the most precarious of existences and his writing reflects that experience. For the second, we use contemporary reports to bring some focus to the activities of self-organised homeless people fighting back collectively against the alienated and oppressive social environment which domi-nates their view of modern Britain.

Leading in, we open with a key report from *Corporate Watch*, looking at the infamous Hostile Environment that Theresa May imposed and how charities were converted into enforcement arms of the Home Office. Through April and May we set the scene of the year's squatting projects before the start of Andrew's diary in June.

As Andrew walked the streets around Ilford and Stratford in London, tent villages were opened against the efforts of Brighton Council to sweep unsightly homelessness away by banning its presence. In Manchester, a vibrant movement took place throughout the year in which homeless people made themselves visible and challenging while the Mayor flailed around with his promises. Campaigns were begun, and won, against charities' co-option into the role of migrant repression. And the book's epilogue, by Tony Martin, offers a deep dive into the decades-long gov-ernment project of disenfranchisement and demobilisation which has built today's crisis. This is a year at the sharp end.

— Rob Ray

INVISIBLE

APRIL 2017

8th | The Hostile Environment

Corporate Watch

This article is part of a larger investigative report looking at the ways the government was trying to discourage "unwanted migration," a policy that would explode into the headlines in 2018 when the Windrush Generation found themselves, after a lifetime of working in Britain, unable to access basic service and care. Of note here was a policy which banned migrants from accessing rented housing. The fully-sourced report can be found at corporatewatch.org

If the renting ban pushes more undocumented people to sleep on the streets, the Home Office's Immigration Compliance and Enforcement (ICE) teams will be waiting for them. Rough sleepers are now a target group for ICE patrols, which rely on close collaboration from local councils, police, and charity "outreach" teams.

Here we summarise some key points from the recent *Corporate Watch* report on this topic, "The Round Up". That investigation focused on London, which has by far the highest concentration of street homelessness in the UK. Similar developments have also been reported in Bristol, Brighton, and other cities with large numbers of rough sleepers.

Immigration Enforcement rough sleeping patrols largely target

European nationals. In London, almost half (47%) of all rough sleepers are non-British Europeans, compared to 41% of British nationals, with smaller numbers from Africa (5.5%) and Asia (4.9%). Particularly large numbers are from Romania (19.5%), Poland (8.7%), and other East and Central European countries which joined the EU in the 2000s. Elsewhere in England, up to 85% of rough sleepers are British.

European Union and other "European Economic Area" (EEA) citizens normally have a right to remain in the UK for 90 days, and indefinitely after that so long as they "exercise their treaty rights": i.e., are working, looking for work, studying, or are independently wealthy. However, in May 2016, the Home Office published a new policy which defines sleeping rough as an "abuse" of treaty rights, making people liable for detention and deportation the first time they are found sleeping on the street. This policy was written into new legislation (Home Office rules) in February 2017.

Under Home Office guidelines, ICE officers have the power to immediately issue a "decision to remove" notice to European rough sleepers, and put them into detention. However, they are supposed to assess whether detention is "proportional". Another option, for example, is that individuals may be supported by homelessness charities to leave "voluntarily". They may also be issued a "minded to remove" letter ordering them to attend a Home Office interview.

A notable feature of this initiative is the collusion of homelessness NGOs and charities, as well as local authorities including the Mayor of London and Greater London Authority (GLA), and local London boroughs. For local authorities, "reconnection" of European migrants is an easy way to make a quick impact on visible homelessness and help meet policy targets.

In central London, local boroughs contract charities to run street outreach services, the first point of contact with rough sleepers. The biggest player is St Mungo's, which runs outreach teams for Westminster, the borough with by far the highest concentration of rough sleepers, and most other central councils. A charity called "Change, Grow, Live" (CGL) runs outreach in Camden and Lambeth. Another, called Thames Reach, runs a mobile outreach programme for most of outer London, contracted by the GLA. St Mungo's also has a GLA programme called "Routes Home," whose role is to "support" migrant rough sleepers identified by the outreach workers to accept "voluntary reconnection". Ten per cent of its fee for this contract is dependent on the number of rough sleepers removed from the UK.

All of these charities routinely work together with Home Office Immigration Enforcement. This collaboration involves three main routes:

- Accompanying ICE officers on joint patrols. Freedom of Information (FOI) responses showed that there were 141 such joint "visits" organised by the GLA and 12 other councils in 2016. Other local authorities, including Westminster, did not respond to FOI requests, and so the full figure will be considerably higher.
- Passing location information on foreign rough sleepers through the "CHAIN" database. This is a London-wide database, commissioned by the GLA and run by St Mungo's, into which outreach teams upload data every night. The GLA then passes CHAIN information onto ICE.
- Liaising with ICE to target individuals who refuse "voluntary reconnection". The outreach teams have agreements in place to hand over information on individuals to ICE for "enforcement" if they have refused to leave voluntarily.

In contrast with some other "hostile environment" policies, the Home Office's "partners" in this sector have themselves been strong advocates of the tougher regime. Westminster Council has said that it "intensely lobbied" for the move to immediate deportation of EU rough sleepers, pushing the policy through a two month pilot with St Mungo's called Operation Adoze, which involved 127 deportations. Much of the new "partnership" approach was developed by a GLA-led body called the Mayor's Rough Sleepers Group (MRSG), in which managers from borough councils, St Mungo's and Thames Reach were active members.

21st | Brighton | The tent village

Freedom News

A homeless camp set up in Brighton on April 5th to protest against a Public Space Protection Order (PSPO) which has been imposed on the city's parks and seafront to discourage rough sleeping was evicted on Wednesday — and activists have responded by taking over a building linked to a £100m development project.

The Circus Street DIY Social Centre has been set up at the city's old university building and squatters are planning to hold it as a radical space and rebuke against the council, which they say is socially cleansing Brighton of its homeless by denying them a place to stay and sleep. In a statement the occupiers, who are involved in campaigns including Raised Fist Collective, Screw the System, Solidarity Federation, Alt SU, Brighton Anti-Fascists and the camp itself, said:

> "We have occupied the space for a number of reasons; firstly, to highlight the wealth of empty buildings across the city, in contrast to the rising problem of homelessness, and as a protest against the draconian new social cleansing law, the PSPO, which criminalises the homeless and traveller communities. We will not leave this

building until this disgraceful, racist and counterproductive law is repealed, and the council opens up empty council buildings to provide shelter to the homeless rather than criminalising them, as they agreed they would at full council on January 26th.

"Secondly, the building has also been occupied, in part, by activists of the Alt SU to show solidarity with Precarious Workers Brighton and to pressure Brighton University, who are guilty of imposing demotions and breaking contracts and agreements with some of the most precariously employed teaching staff in the university. We will not leave this building until the university reverses the demotions of Hourly Paid Lecturers in the School of Computing, Engineering and Mathematics, reinstates the 70% pay cut, pays them retrospectively for work done at the lower rate, and publicly commits to not attempting to enact these demotions again.

"We have been busy turning our new home into a far more positive space than the empty mess we found it in. The space will be used to provide shelter for rough sleepers, and will be used to put on workshops and talks, using the building to educate once again, and to give space for radical groups to come together to share and discuss their politics; a politics which seeks to create a world free from tyranny and oppression, to ensure that no person should go without whilst there is such plenty.

"It is a disgrace and a dismal failure of society that people should go without food or shelter when we waste so much and so many buildings lie empty across the country, simply gathering dust or increasing value for rich oligarchs from around the world, who will never even see the inside of the building they "own". We have more than enough for everyone, and it is these insatiable capitalists — who conquest for ever expanding profits and surplus at the price of every ordinary member of society, and the natural world — who are responsible for the shitstorm we find ourselves in, with rising poverty and brewing climate catastrophe".

The homeless camp, which had been based on land next to St Peter's Church not covered by the council's PSPO, was cleared by police on council orders in an action which campaigners say offered no legislative grounds or paperwork. Activists say they were told earlier in the week that they would be able to stay until the end of the month before it was set up for a festival. The campers said:

> "This is another clear example of those who are supposed to write and uphold the laws abusing their positions of trust and power. When our activists arrived at 9am the homeless had already been evicted and the camp cleared. Apparently they came in at 7.30am. Please share your angry emails and letters with the council and cite your opposition to PSPO".

The camp had, until the eviction, been receiving solid support from local people, who gave everything from sanitary products and sleeping bags to firewood and pin badges. Around 200 people are homeless in Brighton at any one time.

MAY

The Homelessness Reduction Act receives royal assent, due to come into force in April 2018. It requires councils to offer free homelessness advice, earlier support and emergency help regardless of priority. £72.7m is to be allocated towards a three-year funding project for councils to achieve the change. The legislation does not, however, make any comment on the phenomenon of private landlords refusing to accept benefits. In Southwark, London, for example, three-quarters of landlords do so.

2nd | Brighton | Circus Street

Circus Street Social Centre statement

At 7am this morning bailiffs, herded by police broke into our squat and began their eviction process. A process of intimidation and violence that we are all too familiar with now. The same process that they use to systematically harass, bully and assault the homeless community daily on the already dangerous streets that they inhabit.

A homeless resident of the squat, in reaction to losing his home, his bed and his safety climbed onto the roof in a show of protest and solidarity with all other displaced people and those he had shared a home with for the two past weeks. For a few hours we waited outside as bailiffs rampaged through our home with such a vengeance that, in their uniquely gorilla-like fashion, they managed to shower their equally vile and incompetent colleagues with shards of glass.

During the process of this the university management dragged themselves out of the gutter to video our friend, precariously balanced on the edge of the roof, whilst pointing and laughing. Again exposing their arrogance and disdain in the face of poverty, homelessness and everything that isn't money for their own pockets.

At around midday the fire brigade turned up to escort our friend off of the roof, which then proved unnecessary as the bailiffs and police decided to drag him down through the roof light in the ceiling. They arrested him on charges unknown and carted him off to Hollingbury holding cells. Police then began to act in line with their standard tactics, brutalising the remaining protesters in order to clear them from the road, with one officer becoming so irate and violent that their commanding officer made him leave. The sergeant on duty advised us to file a complaint. After this incident and after our friend was carted off to the cells, a small group went to protest at the university, experiencing student care and protection at the hands of the security guards as they choked one activist and threw another to the ground. Our position on the university is this:

The University of Brighton management have consistently exposed their hatred of vulnerable peoples and communities, from women, to the homeless and from survivors to migrants. They have demonstrated this, several times over, and their rhetoric of inclusivity, tolerance and progressive politics is transparent and empty. They have declared war on everyone, bar yuppy students and their bank accounts, and we, the community, will answer.

To the rest of the enemies of the poor, hear this: we have lost this building, but we have gained a network of strength, skills and diversity. A network that will continue, to the end, our struggle; the struggle of those displaced, vulnerable and persecuted communities and peoples. We will continue until we win, and people can sleep safely, eat well and be safe in our city again.

8th | Manchester | The Cornerhouse

Freedom News

After successfully seeing off an eviction last Tuesday, homeless people backed by the Manchester Activist Network (MAN) have made a callout for support in what they say is a "high alert period" in their fight to keep their Oxford Road site open as a centre for the city's regular rough sleepers, the number of which has quadrupled since 2010 to a little under 200 on average.

The former Cornerhouse cinema, which is owned by Network Rail, is slated for eventual redevelopment but has been left vacant for the last two years. In a statement, the group said:

"As the housing climate in Manchester is not changing, we're maintaining our presence in the unused space to offer shelter, support and advice. The need for solutions to Manchester's housing issues is our driving force, and claiming empty buildings is how we share the opportunity for people to come and get involved.

"The future looks full of lost hope, with housing benefit cuts for under-25s, as many more face the uncertainty to find a property and afford to live without vital financial support.

"On March 3rd the government laid regulations before parliament to remove the automatic entitlement to housing costs under Universal Credit for single people aged 18-21. It is expected to affect 1,000 young people in the first year, rising to 11,000 eventually.

"Even those who work over 16 hours a week on low wage will struggle to pay for the increasing price of house rentals. In Britain 35,000 have been on the waiting list for over 10 years, and at present the reality of finding adequate housing fails for young people as the council decide priority based on "the rehousing bands". Age restrictions can also reduce the priority for housing associations, making many of those facing homelessness vulnerable to the environment in the City's hostels, or to sleep rough, if they are unable to find any alternative housing option.

"Manchester Activist Network is here to make a stand against the increase of homelessness whilst the council is blinded by property developers who continue to expand into the market of luxury accommodation. In the past 18 weeks, we have taken direct action to create a community environment that allows for people to come together and mobilise around housing issues. This led to the six-week project Loose Space in the abandoned Cornerhouse Cinema, which has become a safe house for 30+ vulnerable homeless people. By providing shelter, warmth, clothes, food and drink, security, hygiene, advice, support, friendship and love, all for free.

"To keep going forward, MAN need your support, donations and volunteers. Come down to the Cornerhouse or send a message us through the MAN Facebook page.

"What's needed: food / coffee and tea / milk / clothes: men's and women's / shoes / toiletries: men's and women's / cleaning products / bedding / sheets / material / pens / paint / chalk / paper / cheap mobile phones with credit (if possible) / laptop / pallets / chains / sand & cement / angle grinder".

JUNE

A charity event for company bosses attracts global scorn after it puts suited elites into a VR suite designed to replicate the "realities" of homelessness. CEO Sleepout wasn't just about demonstrating how good virtual reality headsets are at making rough sleeping seem real of course, the event also had participating executives do an outdoor sleepover at a cricket ground hired by the organisers.

24th | East London | That hideous sound

Andrew Fraser

It's the constant beeping which is the worst. Mental torture served up by good old Marks and Spencer. I won't be buying my pasties from them ever again. I wonder what Saint Michael thinks of their behaviour.

I was sleeping behind Marks and Sparks in Ilford for a while. Under the tunnel, next to my Polish, Lithuanian, Russian, Portuguese and Romanian brothers and sisters. It's probably the safest place to kip, all told. Whatever our differences we are all in it together, so if someone threatens to knife you to get your mobile phone, or a cigarette, you know you've got back-up. Not that I need it really anymore. I'm good at fronting it with those types and they only tend to pick on the ones who appear mortally wounded. As my good friend Aiden put it, on one of my first days back on the streets, "you cry, you die".

But that hideous sound. I always associated Marks and Spencer with comfort and gentility. My grandma used to take me there as a child and a visit to their food hall was a real joy and a privilege. No more. The beeping starts about midnight, just as you're dropping off to sleep and it continues until around the time that passers-by might notice and alert people to the human cruelty they are inflicting.

It's horrible, and no amount of ear plugs can block it out. Just to twist the knife, they tend to stop it for a while … usually around 3am, and your exhausted body exhales. "Oh thank fuck, it's stopped". But that's just a cruel trick, as you finally sink into a state of sleep, it starts again, about twenty minutes later. It's vindictive beyond words and yet we're causing no bother, we always leave our place under the tunnel clean and tidy. We aren't hurting anybody. We are human beings trying to survive.

In the morning, you awake, dazed from no rest and try to steady yourself, see if you can bring yourself to get your sorry arse to the job-centre, benefits or maybe earn some cash. It's hard when you are sleep deprived. You have to be on top of your thoughts. Just staying alive is a constant battle and you can't afford to make a mistake. But your brain is weary. Luckily it's warm now so you can collapse in Valentine's Park for a few hours if necessary. Valentine's Park is full of people collapsed on the grass. People thrown on life's rubbish heap, like me.

I feel weird today. Maybe it's because I've stopped smoking. Picking up dimps is part of the full-time job of being homeless. But it's such a waste of energy. More likely it's because latterly I've been sleeping under a roof. I've had a shower and a shave, put on clean clothes. Walking down Romford High Street, in my borrowed clothes, I could pass as a "normal" person. Indeed, I actually do. I finally understand the expression "fish out of water" and I feel uneasy. A young cockney black guy approaches me. I'm waiting for him to offer me Spice, but instead he asks me if I think my credit rating is good, fair or bad. I collapse into giggles and he enquires no more. I bet his isn't so good either, kerb crawling for credit card companies on the minimum wage. Still, you do what you have to do to get by.

Then a chirpy Yorkshire lass asks me who my home broadband pro-vider is. It feels odd. Normally the chuggers and gym and mobile data purveyors swerve me. I look too much like what I am. Homeless. But today I must be looking more respectable. Well every cloud has a silver lining and being homeless and looking like shit does, at least stop you getting accosted by chuggers. Again I laugh, I don't get broadband in my sleeping bag I tell her, as gently as possible. She looks aghast. "Noooh, you can't be homeless". I walk off. Oh God, I feel like such a fraud. At the station I see my mate Jamie sitting with his sleeping bag. I give him a few dimps I collected. Old habits die hard. And I can't escape the feeling that I've betrayed him in some way. Survivors' Guilt, I guess. Whatever you want to call it. He tells me he loves me and I reciprocate. I really do, even though I barely know him. I know enough, and I know his story is my story. It's all our stories. Mistakes made, bad calls, betrayal, mocked, abandoned, reborn stronger, lost then found then lost again, booze, fags, whatever else gets you through (though I stuck to the old reliables), disrespect from them, respect for yourself and your street family. Love. Dysfunctional love yes, but a love which runs so deep it manages to cut through the darkest moments.

And now here I am. In Romford. Disguised as someone I used to be. The one who used to walk past. Whatever happens to me from here on in, and only God knows that, I know I can never go back and I truthfully believe I am better for that.

25th | East London | A funny sort of caring

Andrew Fraser

There is a fate worse than homelessness. I pondered this as I looked at the images of charred Grenfell Tower. Now the world's highest cemetery. I know from my own experience, from the experience of my brothers and sisters on the streets, that you are never more in danger than when you are in the "care" of the local housing authority. At least on the streets you are assured that you are not safe and you know to keep your eyes in the back of your head, unlike those poor souls at Grenfell who fell for the lie.

I had a nice room in Newbury Park. After two and a half weeks standing in Waltham Forest Housing with my bags, from 9.30am to 5.30pm, waiting for my "case worker" to come and see me. Paying the transport costs to drag my bags across London, I finally got a place. It was horrible in those queues. You are feeling your own agony but also absorbing the pain of those other poor souls around you. This man was there last time I was in, Somali I think, with his wife. He needed to give the council a photocopy of his passport. He did. Six times. And six times they "lost" it. Now he faced losing his home. He began to cry and shout. DON'T shout. You'll be straight back at the back of the queue. "Where are my human rights?" he screamed. I rubbed his shoulder and told him the truth. "Mate, you don't have any. Get used to it and get ready for the fight of your life".

In those dreadful two-and-a-half weeks I only saw my "case worker" once. She dragged me to reception and asked me to explain my predicament. "I'm homeless, traumatised, frightened to death, occasionally contemplating suicide and now being asked to say all this in front of a long line of people behind me because YOU can't grant me the dignity of a private room in which I can express my distress". She marched off and I never saw her again. But I did get to know the people who worked downstairs. Lovely folk. Human beings. Dan told me I was the joint-nicest "customer" they'd ever had in there. On the 13th day of this ordeal they saw me start to break and, apparently they used the "emergency" word. I was housed that night. And I lived there for five-and-a-half months. Happy times, comparably. Then they moved a Muslim fundamentalist homophobe, one month out of a mental hospital, into the room next door to me. He threatened to kill me because he wasn't so keen on gay people. I wasn't so bothered by that. I'd have kicked his arse. But I refused to live next door to someone who calls me "unnatural". I have many faults, but that's not one of them … I marched down to Waltham Forest the next day, and they rehoused me, in my old manor, Leytonstone. On Bulwer Road.

Back to my old stomping ground. I was happy. It was a hostel but I'm not fussy, so long as people are nice. What they omitted to tell me was that everybody else in the hostel, apart from me, was on crack or smack. On the first night I was up until 5am disarming a crackhead with a knife.

This perturbed me somewhat. I spoke to the manager and asked her to please not put any more drug addicts in my room. That night I met my good friend Gavin and his wife for supper and then went back to the hostel. As I was walking in they were putting a bloke into my shared room. "Is he on drugs?" I asked warily. "No he's a good guy. Look after him," they told me. I did. Several hours later I was disarming a violent smackhead who nicked my mobile phone and lots of my money. On the next night I dragged my bags down to Stratford shopping centre. It was safer there. Most of them down there don't do that shit, hence the fact that they don't get homes.

Grenfell is a horrible indictment of the country I used to call home. Now I largely loathe it. It would be nice to believe that those poor souls who perished on that night, have at least been sacrificed so that some compassion, morality, heck — love — might come into housing policy. But I shan't be holding my breath. At least the Grenfell residents will eventually get a bodycount. There are probably a couple of Grenfells every week across our major cities. People with promise dying needless-ly because of government rules which are not so much parsimonious as vindictive. These deaths will largely go unreported. But as they bury the victims of Grenfell, many others, left for dead by society, will be being slung into unmarked graves from the top to the toe of "Great" Britain.

26th | East London | Life in fear

Andrew Fraser

I woke up crying this morning. Don't normally do that. I'm generally very positive. But something was bothering me and I needed to get to the bottom of it. And it's okay to cry so long as nobody sees it.

I met Saul yesterday and had a lovely couple of hours. He's my mate and a bit of a hero. A gentle giant from Portugal. I bumped into him when I was on my uppers in Ilford. I didn't know it, but I needed him. To cut a long story short, he did his best to take care of me. I had hardly any clothes but he bought me new shoes, trousers, underpants, a t-shirt. So I could feel dignified again.

Just arrived in Romford. Its seriously clammy today. Saw the news about the mosque attack in Finsbury Park. Something's brewing in England and it's shaping up to be a long, hot summer. The Tories are gonna reap the whirlwind. But it's not them who are lying dead. I hope they're scared though. Me and my mates live our lives in fear because of them. I hope, they too, are having sleepless nights.

Anyway, as fate would have it, just as I began to get back on my feet, this government came along and tried to knock Saul off his. He's been homeless before. That's why we understand each other like no one else can. The greatest fear for a street person is being sent back from whence they came. Saul didn't really need to tell me what happened to him. It's in the way he walks. Shoulders back, head held high. Street bravado. But also twitchy. Looking over his shoulder constantly. Scanning the land to look out for danger. I do the same. Whereas I mainline anger to medicate my nerves, he is permanently agitated. No wonder. This country gives him no rest.

He's studying to be a clinical psychologist, working so hard. TOO hard. But he's scared of going back to where he was, understandably. He was doing well. He pulled himself up by his bootstraps and got himself a nice flat in Ilford. I imagine he maybe even exhaled for five minutes. Then the government intervened. They changed the "rules" so that where he was previously entitled to ESA (for his trauma) and housing benefit, now he is no longer. He's left without a penny to his name and facing the fear he might lose his home again. I won't let him go back to the streets.

I don't know what I will do but I won't let that happen. But you see, that's what the government and benefits apparatchiks do. Whole lives destroyed in the stroke of a pen. He can appeal and he will probably win, but what use is backdated money when you have none. He has nothing, and I have next to nothing but I have learned a handy trick. A local supermarket reduces its prices at 3pm on a Sunday. Food they would otherwise throw out. I took him there and helped him fill his freezer. It only came to £9 for enough food to feed us both for the week. So at least I know he's fed. That should help with his anxiety. I saw another side of him yesterday. There was a greedy man grabbing everything he could get, reduced price, shoving people out of the way to get his selfish mitts on the bargains. Looking at his paunch, he wasn't exactly dying of starvation. At one point I thought Saul was gonna hit him and I had to whisper to him to calm down a bit, which is rich coming from me, scourge of doctors' receptionists and canvassing Tory MPs, to name but two. My temper is terrible these days but I'm not seeing my mate arrested over a cut price pie. Anyway, Saul had his moment, barging him out the way to grab some delicious seafood. I'm going to have some when I've finished this. Kromer crab, reduced from £4.83 to 45p. Thank you Saul. I told you he is a hero.

This heat is getting to me. And I'm beginning to annoy myself. Really, my temper is awful. I used to be what one would call "easy going". I'm not anymore. I have zero tolerance for bullshit. That's not grandiosity. It's just what happens when you've been pushed around too much. I just came to the library in Romford, to write this, but my phone was nearly dead so I politely asked the lady behind the counter if they would mind charging my phone. She said it would cost a pound. That's about 3% of what I have left until Friday after next. I asked her why they charged such a huge amount. She shrugged and said "well somebody's got to pay for it". So it costs a pound in electricity to charge a phone for 20 minutes so that

I can phone my social worker and keep up the fight to not lose the place in which I am currently sleeping? Bullshit. It costs a fraction of a penny, common decency and a bit of human kindness.

I digress, as usual. So after seeing Saul I went down to my old local to see my friends, many of whom helped me through some of my darkest days. I was really excited. I haven't been properly out in a month, so it was a treat. One I can't afford but I'll go nuts and sink into depression if I just stay in my room contemplating the fact that I have to live on £4 a day. I'll make up the difference singing up at Newbury Park station tonight. Normally I sing Abba, but tonight it might be Morrissey.

Anyway, once again I had that "fish out of water" feeling. Here I was, among friends, talking about their love lives, mortgages, plans for supper the next day. And I just couldn't fit in. I kept dragging the conversation back to social policy and housing. I am officially a bore. I can't help it. I don't do that with Saul, or with my friends on the street, because I know they already know this stuff. But I just want to shout it so loud. "I don't care about your new teabags, LISTEN to me, people are dying. Tonight". When will this end? When will I fit in again? Did I ever? Really?

And I've lost count of the friends and family who tell me, "we just want the old you back". The amiable one. The easygoing one. I smile and try to act like how I used to act, if I can cast my mind back that far, but there have been a lot of near-death experiences in the intervening period, so it's hard to remember who he was and how he was. And all I really want to tell them, and then give them the option to give up on me and walk away, is the truth. He's not coming back. For better and for worse, he died on the streets of Ilford.

28th | East London | The controversy of giving

Andrew Fraser

This will probably come across as controversial … but who cares? I know what I'm talking about. If you see a homeless man or woman and you feel like helping them, buy them a beer … or better still, give them the money so they can choose whether to buy a beer for themselves, or perhaps they'll go and invest in a hanging basket to tie onto the end of their sleeping bag I dunno. But give them the freedom to choose which they would prefer. My guess is most will opt for the beer.

Shocking huh? Not really. Don't you like a nice cold drink at the end of a long and stressful day? You deserve it, right? Sure you do … it chills you out and helps you switch off from worrying about tomorrow's stresses. It's no different if you're homeless.

How about we turn your perception on its head. It was mine too. "They're on the streets because they drink and take drugs". In most cases, that simply isn't true. But some of them do drink and take drugs BECAUSE they are on the streets.

So the night before, you might have been protecting a girl you just met, who has just landed on the streets, from getting raped in the night by pitching your sleeping bag next to hers. Then you sleep with one eye open for her safety, one eye open for yourself … so you're essentially sleeping with both eyes open,

There was the night I met my Slovakian friend Pieter. He was one of the gentler guys on the street. He spoke little English yet had somehow managed to survive for five years. "Never forget what a strong man you are," I used to tell him. But he didn't look it. My goodness, Pieter liked a drink and I bought him a few tins then lost touch with him for a few nights.

Then I saw him walking down Ilford High Road with tears streaming down his face. Remember, "you cry, you die". I went over to him and hugged him. He looked petrified and totally traumatised. Then this big fucker jumped out of the shadows and came straight for Pieter brandishing a knife. I turned my back on Pieter and faced the guy with my arms out wide to block him from getting near my friend. Pure bravado, with jaw clenched, I shouted "get the fuck away from him" … He did.

Pieter staggered to the bus station and I followed him. I couldn't get any sense out of him but reading between the lines I think there was a homophobic element to the attempted attack, alongside the fact that Pieter was just a bit too gentle for that world. He's 38 but looks at least 15 years older. He drinks too much but who can blame him. The streets of London were not paved with gold for this East European migrant … but they were drizzled with blood.

At the bus station two other guys approached him and I saw him turn even whiter … he ran onto the nearest bus and shouted at me to get on with him. We got on, showing our sleeping bags to the driver who kindly let us on for free, understanding the gravity of the situation. On the bus we went round and round and round in a circle all night until it was dawn, while Pieter quivered like a jelly and I hugged him and repeatedly told him to remember how strong he is. I couldn't let him give up.

At dawn I left him with another beer, bought a couple for myself and staggered to Valentine's Park where I collapsed for a couple of hours. God that drink helped. It really, really helped. A few hours later I was due back in housing, preparing to be routinely insulted and lied to on a fruitless search for somewhere to live so I popped in Tesco Metro on the way, and bought another cider. There is an extremely smug and rude security guard in there who thinks it's cool to insult homeless people. She picked the wrong day and the wrong man.

"You bought your breakfast then?" she scoffed hatefully. My head swivelled, exorcist-stylee and I knew instantly from her expression that she realised she had made a big uh-oh.

"Listen darling, I was protecting a guy from being stabbed last night. A few days previous I was staying up with a girl who was frightened of being raped so if I want a fucking drink I'll have a fucking drink and don't think, just because you are stood there in your smelly uniform, that you are any better than me or any of my mates out there. Because you ain't. You wouldn't last five minutes out there honey, because YOU have no respect".

This was not the response she expected. Nor the other till staff who all took a deep breath. "Now, say you're sorry," I said. Much to my surprise, she complied. "Sorry" she said, not looking quite so big and hard anymore. It wasn't enough. She hadn't just insulted me, she'd insulted my family.

"Because me and my 'tramp' friends pay your fucking wages with our booze purchases," I continued. "You might wanna invest some of your minimum wage on purchasing a deodorant. And get educated love, PLEASE get an education".

I swigged from the bottle triumphantly as I walked from the store. Gargled some mouthwash and headed for housing.

29th | East London | A sudden fall

Andrew Fraser

Bloody Marks and Spencer. I detest them now and I want justice for what they do to homeless men and women, I may need your help with this one …

They're not completely to blame for Josef's death. Not complete-ly. Probably not even mostly. There are a lot of culprits who should be named and shamed. Like *Murder on the Orient Express*, when it turns out they ALL dunnit. That's pretty much true of all the folk on my shit list. But as I walked past their pristine, respectable food court in Ilford today, I spat on the ground.

Josef isn't dead yet, by the way. But as my mate Alan correctly ob-served ... he's a dead man walking.

I first met him on my first night behind Marks and Spencer, where they play the constant "beep, beep, beeping" all night to mentally disturb the people sleeping there. They stop it around 3am, a particular twist of the knife, and you exhale, hoping desperately that you might finally get some rest. It starts again 20 minutes later and and you hear your mates from Romania. Lithuania, Russia, Poland, Portugal and elsewhere col-lectively moan. Apart from the ones who have had so many substances they are comatose. One night I had had enough and it was the anger at the injustice and the cruelty as much as the beeping which kept me from sleeping. I dragged my sleeping bag down to behind the police station and got my head down there for a few hours. It was a dangerous move. Behind M&S, under the bridge, no matter how horrible that sound is, you know you have your mates around you as backup. I was alone be-hind the police station but I'd picked up a brick on the way to defend myself and I was well hidden by the bushes should anyone intrude.

Josef was one of the sensible ones. The others were often more dis-turbed, less mature, more flammable. But he just seemed to get on with it. A cool head on broad shoulders. I felt safer knowing he was there and the fact that he was a good guy shone out of his piercing grey-green eyes. I would always see him on his bike, off looking for work, he didn't drink much, if anything at all, and he would show me his artwork. He was a very talented man.

I didn't see him for a couple of months until I was walking through Ilford a few weeks back and I saw an ambulance stretchering a man off the streets. It was him. I couldn't believe my eyes. He appeared flat-out drunk. His street friends gathered to try and get him to come-to and eventually he was driven away to hospital. I prayed the rest might do him good. At least he had a bed and shelter and he would be away from that infernal beeping.

I saw him today. I really have to avoid going through Ilford because when I see my street friends I inevitably give away more of my time, money and food than I really can afford at this moment. But it's impossible to walk by. I love these people and I could so easily be him.

His face was all puffed up and his shoulders sunken, a shadow of the man I used to sit and chat about his art with, just a few weeks ago. I made him a sandwich out of the reduced-price sausage and bacon and bread I had packed in my bag for lunch. And then a second one because he hadn't eaten for two days. He was incoherent and crying. I said "This isn't like you Josef!" He said, "it isn't me. it's my twin brother". I told him I don't recognise him and to please see a doctor urgently. I told him I'd take him to a hospital but he had other plans.

He told me he is seeing visions. He sees flashes before his eyes. Later I found out that him and many of his friends from Eastern Europe have started drinking Ethanol for £1 a litre. They will be blind, then dead, within weeks.

So why did my sensible friend suddenly lose the plot and decide to self-destruct? Why did a thoroughly calm and intelligent man break and decide to give up on everything? Why was he mentally disturbed in the first place?

Sleep deprivation is a terrible thing and I'm pointing the finger at you Marks and Spencer. Sure, you didn't actually come along and bludgeon him to death with a spade. But you may as well have done. If you still feel like enjoying M&S's frou-frou food court delights, feel free. But frankly today put me off their prawn cocktail butties forever.

If people who ignored safety rules are responsible for the manslaughter of those who died in Grenfell Tower, then dear old Marks are responsible for the mental deterioration of my good friend and now his inevitable, eventual death, they are responsible for the rapes of girls who leave the safety of the commune behind their store and get attacked in the park, the people like myself who may have got stabbed because they took themselves off to somewhere unsafe to save their sanity from that horrible, horrible din.

I know it's not just Ilford where they are doing this. If you care about this, I want you to help me organise a boycott of Marks and Spencer until this human crime against people who are doing no harm, and always tidy up after themselves. I contacted them and they flat-out refused to apologise and stop.

It's funny, but the guy who set up Marks and Sparks in Leeds, all those years ago was an immigrant, just like the people they mentally torture outside their stores.

I'm tired of hand-wringing. Please help me get justice for my friends. Help me get this stopped.

JULY

Housing charity Cymorth reports on its investigation into the link between a lack of healthcare access and homelessness. A third of rough sleepers interviewed said health problems had contributed to them losing their homes. Nearly a quarter reported being discharged back onto the streets.

24th | East London | List of Impossible Things

Andrew Fraser

Crazy the mystic's song
But what if they're right all along?
Trust what you cannot know
And pray 'til your prayers make it so.

Where to start?

Just for once, I won't start with me.

My mate Mark was living on the street for a year. His beautiful wife has a disability. He's ex-army. A brave and proud man. They should never have been living on the streets. But they had to. I'll get back to why later.

Anyway, one night, someone thought it was funny to throw a firework at Mark's wife, Michelle. It exploded as he stamped on it. There was no burn. Nothing. A miracle.

Back to me, haha. Several weeks ago, I was in Valentines Park, Ilford, looking for a Holy Well. I had to find it, an amazing lady called Maureen Rolls told me to. You see I'd been cursed. By something very bad. I woke up one morning, in Georgia, the Caucasus, with a weird burn on my right foot. I was concerned. Someone I don't know, told me to call Maureen. I did. But after about two minutes the line went dead. I'd run out of credit. I'd just topped up my phone. It didn't make sense. But then, at that point, nothing in my life was making sense. It does now.

She called back. She told me not to be scared. That something was interfering with our call. I was crying at this point. I was so exhausted. It's been a long and bumpy ride. She gave me a prayer and told me to find this Holy Well.

I didn't have a clue how to find one, so I Googled 'Holy Wells near you', as you do. Lo and behold, there's a website that lists them, and there's one in Valentine's Park.

So I satnavved my way there. I didn't have credit on my phone, so I had to sit outside McDonald's to find it.

I got to the park, with no clue where to look. It's a big park.

I had literally no idea what to do, so I sat against an old oak tree and I prayed. With all my heart, I prayed.

Anyway, I looked up, and pretty much opposite there was a guy sitting with his head in hands, looking sad. I was magnetised toward him, so off I went launching myself again, into the world.

He had his eyes closed, but next to him was a book. It was called Steps to Christ. I tapped him on the shoulder, and asked if he was okay. He played me a sad song and told me the book was for me. He was VERY drunk. Even drunker than me. But I comforted him, and told him of my crazy mission, to find this sacred well.

He knew where it was, and as he smoked and drank and laughed, I bathed my right foot, as I had been instructed. We sat by the duck pond, as geese gathered, and he offered me a cigarette. I said "No thank you, I can't give you one back. I have no money. I'm broke." He reached into his pocket and brandished a £20 note. I said, I can't take that. He insisted. I said I would only take it, if he gave me his number and let me call him to give it back. He refused. He said, pass it on. I did of course. I'll tell you later how.

He wanted to go on his way, so I cleaned up his whisky bottle and cigarette dimps and put them in my bag. He said goodbye, not before telling me the way home. I looked around to wave and he had gone. Disappeared. I walked to the end of the street he sent me to, looking for a bin, to dispose of his whisky bottle and dimps. Next to the bin there was a bag, with two clean pillows. I needed clean pillows since I had become homeless. This is the list of impossible things.

9th | Manchester | Burnham's promise

Freedom News

New Manchester Mayor Andy Burnham's pledge to help street homeless people as a major plank of his candidacy seems to have gone off the rails after his office failed to actively respond to protests over the eviction of a self-organised occupied space in the centre of the city.

Around 40 people squatting at the Hotspur Press building off Whitworth Street were violently evicted and made homeless earlier this week, shortly after Burnham had called on private businesses to open the doors of vacant plots to alleviate the city's rising street homeless crisis.

The building, which has maintained strong links with the more publicly-known Cornerhouse Cinema squat, was a major support space for the homeless community and its eviction prompted a protest on Thursday which included a slow walk on Burnham's office — the mayor has recently been busy with his "digital Manchester drive".

But as footage captured by Established Beyond showed, while protesters gathered in solidarity with the squatters, who have been made homeless on the street with their belongings, an agitated attending police officer reacted violently to the situation. Officer 2553 can be seen dragging a woman across the street in a headlock. Other activists were quick to try help her, but little could be done against a barrier of bailiffs. In a statement, Manchester Activist Network said:

> "The solution is not through bailiff force and police arrests over a building that has provided shelter for 40 people. Yesterday's actions only succeeded in making more people homeless, with unnecessary and violent arrests of peaceful protesters".

And Greater Manchester Housing Action said:

"This is not the kind of action this city needs to address its ongoing housing crisis. "The squatting of empty buildings is often a last resort for desperate people, unable to find a secure home due to a devastating lack of secure tenancies, decent housing and stable employment opportunities. By evicting squats, the police, bailiffs and council are only serving to make the situation worse for people with nowhere else to go.

"The city of Manchester has a well documented homelessness crisis, which has its origins in policy decisions made at both a national and city level. An unwillingness by council leaders to build the social housing that people need, the slashing of homelessness support due to austerity, and the damaging changes to the benefits system brought in by the Coalition government are all factors which have led to this crisis.

"We condemn the eviction and stand in solidarity with those who have just been made homeless. We believe that turning 40 more people onto the streets in order to prepare the ground for luxury redevelopments is not the solution, and instead call for renewed construction of social housing, action to cap rent in the private sector and make long term tenancies the norm and a housing first approach to the homelessness crisis".

14th | East London | The controversy of giving

Andrew Fraser

Even the mundane days are eye-opening when you're in the gutter.

I went to the Welcome Centre for lunch yesterday feeling a bit downhearted and rejected, it's a fairly common feeling if you've been on the streets. It's hard to trust human beings again and sometimes you can be your own worst enemy, pushing people away before they get the chance to let you down. But in this instance, I kinda had been rejected again. Hey ho, who hasn't?

But before I even got to their glass doors I saw Dumitru jumping for joy, literally leaping in the air when he saw me approaching. It was a lovely feeling. On one of my first nights back on the street he made me a bed and I will never forget that. He speaks hardly any English and I speak no Romanian but we somehow understand each other and love each other to bits. He's tricky. He has a serious temper but then so do I. That's what happens when you get pushed around too much. He channels it into his boxing.

One day, when I was still smoking, I was sitting outside Morrisons in Dagenham, having a fag and talking to my friend about meditation. Oh the irony. This gym-muscled geezer came out the shop and walked over to his fancy motor. "Bro!" he yelled. "Give us a cigarette!"

No please. No excuse me. And I couldn't remember the day I nominated him as being one of my numerous brothers. In fact, I'd never met him, he was just a stupid person looking for a free cigarette who actually thought I was so thick that I would give him one because I would feel guilty at turning down my "brother"…

I didn't flare up straight away. I was talking about meditation after all. "'I'm sorry, I'm on the phone to my friend. And I'm homeless," I told him, assuming, wrongly, that that would be an end to matters.

"Well you shouldn't be smoking a cigarette then should you," he said puffed up with self-righteousness.

"Excuse me?" I said, leaping to my feet. "Who the fuck asked you? As it happens, Theresa May bought me a packet of cigarettes out of my paltry benefits. I know I really shouldn't but I'm a bit stressed, what with trying not to get stabbed every night and shit. And anyway, who the fuck are you, in your fancy car, poncing cigarettes off homeless people?"

"Well you don't look homeless!"

"That's 'cos I had a shower and I put on clean clothes," I told him. "What do you want me to do, roll in the mud so that YOU, whoever YOU are believes that I'm homeless".

You could almost hear the penny dropping as I pulled a cigarette out of my packet and launched it across the car park. It was a perfect shot, hitting him smack in the middle of his forehead. To my eternal amusement, he picked it up off the floor.

"You really are homeless?" he said…

"Yes!"

"Are you sure you want me to smoke this?"

"Yes! I want you to smoke it real slow my friend and while you smoke it think about engaging your brain before you open your big fat stupid mouth and insult another person about whom you know nothing. And just for the record, I ain't your brother. I'm picky".

"You take care of yourself," he said, looking sheepish.

"Like you care," I growled under my breath.

It doesn't always wind up negatively with my temper. One night I was in O'Neill's having a pint. It was one of those weeks when I actually had a bit of spare money. I had no passport so I couldn't get anywhere to sleep, but I did have a little spare cash. I had my bed in a bag on the stool next to me.

"Who's left their washing out?" scoffed this northern bloke who just walked in, "Oi! That's my bed! Don't be rude!" I snapped. He turned out to be really nice, a funny bloke and a real gentleman, called Paddy, he bought me a couple more pints and let me bring my bed into the tiny space he was sleeping in around the corner while he worked on the construction sites for a pittance. I haven't seen him since but I do hope karma has rewarded my brother Paddy.

Back to yesterday, and I walked back to the bus stop, via the bridge where Dumitru and the others sleep. I thought I'd surprise him with some cider and a sarnie. He's a tough character, a kickboxer, but yesterday I saw him cry for the first time. He'd had a shit day. I don't think it was anything in particular, just that accumulation of hopelessness when you feel like you've just wasted another day trying to climb up a ten foot pole which has been greased by the government. Trying to achieve the impossible and get yourself out of this hole. You know the odds are massively against you, that there is probably no chance of escaping, but the will to stay alive keeps you going. Until it doesn't.

I've been there before when he has contemplated doing bad things to himself. I hope he never does. I hope some miracle comes along and pulls him out of this mess because I don't have the power to do that. He truly is my brother. When I sat down next to him he made the sign of the cross and looked upstairs and said "thank God". I gave him a cuddle because no-one was looking. I hope he made it through another 24 hours.

18th | East London | Priya

Andrew Fraser

It's getting harder to venture into Ilford. I always cry at some point, just so long as no one is looking. But usually it takes an hour or two. Today it happened as soon as I stepped off the bus.

Perched on top of a bin was Priya, looking scrawnier than ever. Last time I saw her she wolfed down three hot meals in half an hour. She's not eating ... and it's fairly obvious where what little money she manages to get hold of is going. On her bony chest she'd stuck a sticker "New hot girls". It was like one of them stickers they put on the reduced price aisle in Tesco, just before the meat goes off.

"You got any food mate?" she asked me, as she always does. I didn't have any but I did give her a quid and a hug. I probably should have spent it on food, because I know the chances are it will go on either crack, smack or Spice. I have no idea which one she is using but I've watched this pretty, feisty, kind-hearted girl decline over the last few months. Now it's accelerated at one helluva pace, after she broke up with her partner. If or when she dies, no doubt her family will be summoned and everyone will stand around and stroke their chins and console themselves that it was "inevitable".

But was it? Was it really? The longer you are left out to die on the streets, the tighter the knot becomes and, yes, untangling it becomes a nigh-on impossible task. But given time, resources, love under-standing — and My God — a home, there should be nothing inevitable in the death of this young girl. She will need a team of people on her side, fighting for her, being an advocate for her, listening to her and sometimes shouting at her. But no, it's not impossible. But Priya knows just as well as I do, that she's already been written off as a lost cause. And if everybody else does that to her, why shouldn't she do the same?

Having shed my tears I walked to the library to avoid my friend Martin. He's been on the crack pipe for several months now, after years of only touching the odd lager. I saw him collapsed on his bed with some hangers-on the other night, the people who no doubt sold him that shit in the first place. I told them to fuck off. Parasites. But then Martin is becoming a parasite now too. These people can drain you of every penny and every drop of positivity that you possess. This lovely African lady offered to feed and house him, get him some rehab and eventually work towards getting him a job. He agreed but when she came to collect him, he was not there. He's a slave to the pipe now.

And yet, this is not the whole story. Most of my brothers and sisters on the street, even now, don't do crack, smack, Spice or (God forbid!) ethanol. They are the strong ones. But the "system" will penalise you for your strength. If you abuse these drugs you tend to get fast-tracked into accommodation. If you don't, you are deemed strong enough to survive, and left out to die. Or after months and years of fighting to get a roof over your head, you one day realise "it ain't ever gonna happen" — so you partake. What the hell? If you can't beat 'em, join 'em.

I had the dubious pleasure of two nights in a "hostel" on Bulwer Road in Leytonstone full of these people. I was the only person in there not doing crack or smack. They omitted to tell me of the danger I was in. Over those two delightful nights I was robbed of my money and my mobile phone, and stayed up for two nights in a row disarming two different blokes who got paranoid and potentially violent, one with a knife. After two days I told "Saint" Mungo's, the "charity'" that put me there, to stick it, and went to sleep down Stratford Shopping Centre. On returning to my old address last week, there was a letter from Waltham Forest, who had dumped me in that shithole, demanding council tax for the period I was on the streets because of them. They have already added £400 in charges because I didn't respond to their letters. They don't deliver post behind the Ilford Marks and Spencer. I should be suing them, seeing as I nearly lost my life because of their cruelty and recklessness. Anyway, in the words of Her Majesty's amoral and duplicitous Foreign Secretary, they can whistle for it.

21st | Bristol | No sympathy at all

Freedom News

A homeless woman's possessions were burnt in front of her by Kingswood arsonists. A friend said people targeted local woman Jo because she is transgender and lives outside. They set fire to her clothing and duvet while she was in church. In the comments section of the local press website, Tracey07 says: "This is a bus stop not a home for the homeless, normal people will have to wait in the rain now for a bus. No sympathy at all … get a job".

22nd | East London | Sleepwalking in Ilford

Andrew Fraser

My thoughts, amid the fog of exhaustion, were "Well if I die tonight at least I die fighting. Not being slowly driven to insanity by sound". At least this way I had my fate in my own hands. Anger also propelled me when at 2am I shouted "fuck you" to the back entrance of Marks and Spencer, Ilford gathered up my sleeping bag and my suitcase and escaped the infernal all-night beeping perpetrated by Britain's cosiest high street retailer against homeless people. I WAS prepared to die that night. I knew the risks. But I wasn't prepared to die on my knees. And on my way to sleep in the doorway around the front of M&S, I grabbed a brick to keep by my side just in case. Someone tried to nick my stuff when I got up a few hours later for a piss but I was quick enough to chase him off.

I was reminded of that brick yesterday, when I met Sara begging outside McDonalds in Ilford, a pretty girl, with a peachy complexion and soft blonde curls. She was soon joined by her boyfriend Jason. They were both on the streets but were happy because they were off to get Sara's first pregnancy scan, later that afternoon. They had only been in Ilford a few weeks and I suggested they might be safer in Romford or Leytonstone where there is at least a community around you to protect you if you are harassed by junkies or police with little regard for the letter of the law, or the niceties in implementing it.

They had had an awful morning, down the housing office. I immediately felt their pain having gone through the same humiliating experience, but this one was shocking even by the standards of London Housing Authorities.

They had gone there in the faint hope that the fact that Sara is pregnant might speed up the process of being housed. They were told by a woman that they were not priority because their baby is not "viable"' until she is 24 weeks pregnant, in a month's time. "How dare she say my baby is not viable," grimaced Sara. I told them not to spend any money on food and to go to the Sikh temple where they will feed you all day, delicious vegetarian dishes, providing you take off your shoes, wear a bandana and behave respectfully. I can't tell you how comforting that place was to be when I went there after being sonically tortured by Marks and Spencer. It felt like someone actually loved me and did mind if I died. God bless the Sikhs.

I asked for their number but they had had their mobile stolen by a gang of young men brandishing bricks. They had managed to sneak into Valentine's Park because it's quieter and nicer than sleeping in a shop doorway. But they told me that many of the girls sleeping up there had been raped in the night by gangs. Now that's too horrible for words and defiling not just the people but also such a beautiful, spiritual, timeless place. I pray the trees don't have eyes and I thought of troubled Priya. Many of those people will have gone there to escape the beeping.

It sometimes feels like everybody is against you, bitches in housing, gangs of kids, Marks and Spencer, GPs and the DSS. And of course the Metropolitan Police who are apparently understaffed yet seem to find plenty of time to harass people who are simply fighting not to die. Sara and Jason had been given a tent. More and more homeless people are turning to this solution. It gets you out of Marks and Spencer's hair, and there are tons of green spaces all over the city where you could pitch up. But this lovely young couple confirmed what I have been hearing from many of my homeless friends. If the police catch you in a tent they will take it away and destroy it. "These Special Police came up to us and said that they were gonna come looking for us after the park shut and this horrible one said that if he found us, he would rip up our tent with his bare hands".

At least Sara and Jason have each other. That must be comforting when you wake up and realise you have countless enemies who will happily grind their boots into your fingers as you try to cling on for dear life. I hope they got to the Sikh Temple and Sara managed to eat for two.

28th | East London | Moment of karma

Andrew Fraser

I remember the first time I went begging. I wasn't homeless. Not all homeless people beg and not all "beggars" are homeless. By the way, I detest the word "beg" but I will use it for these purposes. I prefer to say, "asking for help".

I was living in temporary accommodation in Newbury Park. It was nice. But the DSS had stopped my benefits. They claimed they hadn't received my medical notes to process my ESA claim. I remember how carefully and meticulously I filled in the dozens of pages of that application form and how I checked and rechecked three times that everything was in the prepaid envelope before I popped it in the post. I remember thinking, "How the hell does anyone manage to do this if they are mentally impaired or trying to do it in a foreign language". It took me a week to decipher those forms but I did it and I got everything in on time.

So it was something of a shock to me, on the day my benefits were due, to discover that there was sod all in my account. I walked to the job centre, a few miles away, because I couldn't afford the bus. I knew the people in there well, the ones downstairs are nice. It's not their fault the system is bent. They taught me an invaluable lesson. Never, ever, ever post anything in a prepaid envelope to the DWP. Things get "lost". "Is it deliberate"' I asked? "Well it happens to everyone, so what do you think?" one person replied. Good point, well made.

I had to go and get another copy of my medical notes. Borrow £10 from a friend (walk to his house to get it) then walk to my financially struggling GP and pay her £10 so she could print off those few sheets of paper. Then walk back to the job centre, several miles away, and get them to scan my medical certificate and send it direct, so they couldn't pretend not to have received it.

In the interim, I had no money. None. At all. For two weeks. Now I'm resourceful, but this was ridiculous. I was still smoking back then. It's hard to give up smoking when your life is precarious. You're stressed and afraid. Anyway, I used to go up to Newbury Park station and pick up dimps (dog ends) and smoke them. On a nice day you could get enough to last you all day. Some people threw away cigarettes where they had barely taken a puff. Imagine that. They must be millionaires!

But now, faced with the fact that I had literally nothing, I had to do something. Obviously my desire to smoke like a chimney was sky-high, because I was stressed to fuck. My housemate Mick was an ex royal-marine, his wife a strong, strong, woman. They had been there and were being fucked around by benefits too. None of us had any money. I knew what I had to do and I knew Mick and Michelle had done the same, so that comforted me as I set off to do it for the first time. If they could do it, so could I. "Never forget who you are and why you are doing this," Mick told me. "It's not your fault". Michelle added: "It takes a strong man to beg". Still, I was petrified.

They had bought me a can of cider so I sat outside McDonalds and knocked it back and put on my Spotify shuffle, hoping for inspiration. As I pulled myself up to go do it, the song 'Begging Me', by Florrie, came on. There were about 250 songs on that playlist. I laughed out loud. God really does have a sense of humour and I know it when I experience it. I winked up at the stars and went and got it over with. My cardboard sign said, "please help". If anyone asked if I was homeless, I explained that I wasn't but that I had no money. I didn't want to be taking money under false pretenses.

Down on the pavement you really get to experience the world as it is. You see the best and worst of human life. Now, I laugh at the horrible ones, but back then, it really was shocking. Some people hated me for having nothing and were not afraid to tell me to my face. Fortunately I also experienced the kindness of strangers, the most wonderful kindness of all. People who gave, and didn't ask questions. They had maybe been there themselves, or maybe just understood that I would hardly have been sitting there for fun. I remember the kind brown eyes of the mixed race guy who gave me my first quid and I quietly sobbed. It was truly humbling. Seeing me crying, I was then hastily given a few more quid by other lovely people. Result! The young 'uns are the best. That really gives you hope for the future. I've always given my money away, when I've had it. Perhaps recklessly. I know my family think so. But I prefer to believe that it stood me in good stead when I needed help from strangers.

Months earlier, I had been that stranger handing out help. What goes around comes around.

When the council effectively threw me out back on the streets a few weeks later, I was back up at the station. Not "begging" now. But singing. I have a decent voice. More of a mournful lilt, these days. I sing 'Don't Give up' by Peter Gabriel and Kate Bush, and 'Money, Money, Money' by Abba, which always makes people laugh. By singing, I'm not technically committing the crime of vagrancy, so the police can't throw me in a cell, as much as I'm sure many of them would like to.

I also make people laugh a bit, just say funny, silly things. This one Saturday afternoon, when I was REALLY screwed, I was singing 'Dancing Queen' by ABBA when this lovely Asian guy came past. "Mate, I'd give to you, but I only have my credit card," he said. "Don't worry my friend," I told him. "Anyway, you wouldn't want to see where I swipe it". He laughed out loud and disappeared to get his train.

Then this bony white woman appeared, literally a hurricane of bad energy, talking cod Posh. She stood above me as I sat on my sleeping bag. "Get a fucking job" she screamed at me.

I leapt to my feet. "I'm fucking singing. I'm not hurting anyone. Who asked you? Mind your own business".

Then she poked her finger real close to my nose staring deep into my eyes. "Get a fucking job, you're a disgrace!" she reiterated.'

I'd had enough. "If you don't remove your nasty finger from my face I swear I will break it off, love". I told her.

She, wisely, left. Would I have done? I hope not, but maybe. You can only take so much being bullied and pushed around. As she left she she roared. "Fack Orrrrf!" And I finally laughed and scratched my head. "Classy bird, aintcha?" I shouted back.

It felt good, to stand up for myself. But I won't pretend I wasn't disturbed and hurt by the experience. I also thought of all the other

homeless people, less able to defend themselves than I, who she will undoubtedly have done this to. One day, she WILL surely lose a finger.

Anyway, I took a deep breath and sat back on my sleeping bag, not
really feeling in the mood to sing. Within minutes the nice Asian guy
came trotting back down the stairs. "Mate, you really made me laugh
there," he said, handing me a £20 note.

As he left, I serenaded him with 'Karma Chameleon'. I hope he's having a great time tonight, wherever he is.

31st | East London | Behind a door

Andrew Fraser

I recently found a safe place to sleep, for now. A room with a roof and
a door and a key and a lock. I felt relieved. Then (and I swear this is life
trying to teach me something) the lock inexplicably broke. I got it fixed
but I don't like sleeping in an unlocked room. Funny that, considering
that I spent countless nights sleeping in the ultimate unlocked room.
Outside. Then I went to the toilet in my favourite pub last night. As I
shut the door, much to my dismay, the handle fell off. Inside and outside.
Instead of being locked out (as usual) I was locked in. Oh the irony.

Us outsiders, we are always either locked out or in. As awful as being
on the streets was, I would always pick that over prison. I was chatting to
a friend the other day, whose brother is in the nick. He's worried. British
jails are flooded with drugs. It's the same as being on the streets, an
outdoor prison. It is beyond easy to score drugs in Ilford. You can do it
from right outside the police station. I never touched them when I was
on the streets but I've seen people smoking crack pipes, yards from Her
Majesty's Constabulary. If you cracked open a can of lager, they would

confiscate it, if they saw you. If you cracked open two, they would arrest you. But they let people take the hard stuff, crack, smack and spice, on the streets and in prisons. Don't you think that's strange, given that they never miss a trick. Just another dead junkie, eh? Some would say genocidal. Either way, I prefer being locked out to being locked in.

London feels like a prison now. So does Britain, since Brexit and the rise of the right. After I left my local I popped into Wetherspoons. Architects of Brexit, they don't let homeless people use their toilets. Even before I was made homeless myself I used to nick their ketchup and give it to homeless people. Call it my little rebellion.

Anyway last night I got chatting to these three Russians. I used to love London's diversity but seriously if there is one country more fucked up than America in this world, it's Russia. The men, in particular, love the muscle flexing of Putin. It's beyond childish that international politics has been reduced to the comparative strength of handshakes of Putin, Trump and Macron. We are being "led" by small boys. Oh and don't forget that witch in Westminster.

Anyway one of the three decided to reveal himself as a bona fide Nazi. He picked up on the fact that I'm not that way inclined. He told me of how he believes gay men and lesbians should be gassed. Laughed as he described what he believes is the impending fate of black and asian people and how, he is quite sure, these people have ruined Britain.

I listened imperviously, smiling politely. Once upon a time I would have told him to fuck off. But I didn't give him the satisfaction of attempting to kick my head in. He wouldn't have anyway. Like most Nazis, he's all bluff and bluster. But what's the point? He's evil. I know it. But seriously he's an amateur compared to some I have come up against. And it really is laughable. Like Theresa May and Donald Trump and his beloved Putin, he thinks he's winning. He thinks he's taking the piss out of us. But one day, he will die. As we all will and he will go somewhere else. And I very much believe that me and him are heading in opposite directions. And should that be the case, I will be surprised if he's laughing then.

I couldn't afford it but I'd missed my last bus so I had to grab a taxi. As I got in, I was told to pay the fare up front. Now, that's just a short way of someone calling you a thief. I'd experienced it too many times when I looked really grubby on the streets. A security guard in Sainsbury's banned me from even looking at their shitty merchandise. I wasn't even allowed to glance in the direction of their nasty pasties. I never shoplifted. Anyway, suffice to say, the driver didn't get a tip. And acknowledging my own hypocrisy, I have just admitted that I did steal ketchup from Wetherspoons and gave it to homeless people. And mint sauce. And mango chutney. Oh well, if you're gonna steal, be Robin Hood.

AUGUST

Welsh government figures suggest a spiral of rising trouble for house-holds will raise the number of homeless people in the country by a third. Around 11,000 people in Wales were classed as homeless in 2016-17 with 300 people sleeping rough. Some 200 households were in "unsuitable" accommodation and 600 in squats, women's refuges, night shelters and tents.

4th | East London | Stay in the Light

Andrew Fraser

When I'm sleeping outside I am so on the ball, so adrenalised. Even with no sleep, so alert. I swear I could plan and direct the invasion of Belgium or Bhutan before breakfast. Not that I'd particularly want to. But the survival instinct is strong in me. All my instincts are.

When I'm homeless, I become feral again — completely obeying my gut. You become closer to your animal self. At least, I did. I could and can smell danger and disingenuousness. I KNEW the last time I became homeless, that it was about to happen, before it happened. This gift saved my life many times. It's God given and we all have that ability, we've just tuned out of it because of the opium that is the banality of modern life. It saved my life many times and we ignore our instincts at our peril. Sometimes I infuriate the people in my life who still love me, by not doing the "logical" thing. I appear stubborn. But when I feel that "punch" in the gut, which says a big resounding no, or tells me to get the hell out of somewhere, even if it doesn't make sense to other people, or myself, I try to go with it. A leap of faith. Once or twice I've allowed myself to be emotionally blackmailed into ignoring that tug and, of course, it ended in disaster, for everyone concerned. Usually the magnetic pull towards something, or the screaming need to get away from something, is so strong, I really have no choice in the matter.

We should all be like street dogs. My mate, Big Baz, has been on the streets for thirty years, so he knows a thing or two about sussing people out before they even open their mouths. But even he can fall for a sob story, or a pretty face, or one of those people who just instinctively home in on your Achilles heel. Luckily for him, he has a Labradoodle called Reginald. Reg is a leg(end). If he notices a wound or an injury on your skin, he will kiss it better with his antiseptic doggy licks. That's if he likes the cut of your jib. If a wanker or a charlatan comes along, Reggie's lovely grey powder puff tail stops wagging. He doesn't get aggressive. He just turns his back and glances away disdainfully. Reginald can't be bought with dog biscuits. He is like a guide dog to us blind mere mortals who have undiscovered our innate ability to trust what we feel and see what is right under our noses.

When I sleep inside, as I have been recently — I'm kind of the opposite. I think it's a reaction to having lived on my nerves for so long. I am usually hyper vigilant these days. But sleeping under a roof allows you to relax a little. I can't linger in bed, because then anxiety and bad memories start to creep in, so I leap out the door — and sometimes I could forget my head, if it wasn't screwed on.

I became homeless three times in the last year. Between the first and the second time I lived in a nice house, sharing it with Mick and Michelle. Building me a home, thinking I'd be strong there. Then Waltham Forest Housing and "Saint" Mungo's intervened, and I was thrown back to square one, only worse. It was deliberate. I'd been blogging about their policies and about how it isn't really a charity, but actually a front for the Home Office, deporting people against their will from Gatwick Airport. I nearly lost my life three times in three consecutive days and every single time, "Saint" Mungo's were directly involved. Of course, I can never prove it, but that's fairly unlucky by any standards. I should have kept my big mouth shut, huh? I probably should now, too. But I do believe the old adage, tell the truth and shame the devil.

Mick, an ex-Royal Marine, who fought for his country — must have sensed that I wasn't going to be there for too long, because he kept teaching me survival skills. He knew a lot having spent a year on the streets himself, with Michelle, who had suffered a stroke and become disabled as a result of their experience. He knew how vindictive the authorities can be. For the first time in my life, he taught me to look after my bodily needs. To listen to what my body was saying.

I'd be rushing out the door, not feeling great and not really sure how I was going to cope with whatever acrobatics the government expected me to perform on that particular day, to stay alive, under a roof. "Have you eaten?" he would say. "Oh, shit, no! I forgot".

Gradually I learned to do it for myself, whenever I had that lingering sense that I'd forgotten to do something important. Like when people think they've left the oven turned on, or the window open. So I learned to listen to myself before I left the house. Have you eaten? Yes. Have you listened to Abba? Yes (I need my uplifting music to raise my vibrations). Have you said thank you to the Universe? Yes. Have you been to the toilet. Yes! (sometimes I would forget this must fundamental need in my race to get out and about, only to find I had to race back home after I had walked halfway down my street, to complete my ablutions.)

I remember one day racing off somewhere and then stopping to pause on the doorstep. Something was wrong. 'What have you forgotten to do?' I KNEW there was something, but I went through my list and really couldn't work out what it was. I went back to my room and perched on the bed. "What can it be?" I thought, feeling suddenly really weary. Then I worked it out. I'd forgotten to sleep.

But there is one human need that is up there with sleep, food, prayer, Abba, ablutions. Crying. I've felt it all week. That dull ache our bodies send us when we know when we have neglected an essential need. It's no use watching comedy to try to cheer yourself up when your body needs to cry. You have to let the pain out, or it will turn in on itself. You have to release the poison.

I once took anti-depressants for four years which basically stopped me from crying, which, I guess, cosmetically, made me seem better. I wasn't. I was in so much need of releasing those chemicals that it drove me to the point of a breakdown. It is good and natural to cry. To be alive is to experience joy but also to grieve. The more awake you are, the more you grieve and the more joy you experience.

That's especially true of us homeless people. We've gone past the point of no return. We can't "tune out" anymore. We can't pretend that Ilford isn't a shithole and walk through with blinkers on. Or pretend that racism and violence and lack of brother or sisterhood and poverty and bullying and murder and rape and abuse of power isn't rife, because we have seen it, vividly, with our own eyes. We LIVED the reality. The one they try to sweep off the streets so that y'all will vote Tory. We CAN'T now unsee the reality of this twisted society.

As a man, I don't feel ashamed of my tears. I remember one day meeting Mick and Michelle in the pub, summonsed by Michelle. Mick had been acting all weird, in his energy. Like he was angry with me. Angry with all of us. As the third wheel in that particular house she was determined to get me involved in getting it out in the open. I'd always known how strong he was, he gave me snippets of what he went through, fighting for his country, truly horrific. Usually he was a vision of calm, but I'm not so daft as to believe that anyone who has lived our lives, any lives, can be like that all the time.

He'd been keeping up a front. To be protective I guess, and also not to show weakness. It's very, very important not to show weakness when you are on the streets and I'm sure, in the trenches (which are not as dissimilar as you might imagine). But we all need to be weak sometimes. Conversely, that reveals true inner strength. It's just knowing that you can do it safely. Around people you can trust. Mick was (not so) secretly devastated. His country had betrayed him.

Many people who he thought were there for him, just weren't. And for risking his life for an ideal, of "Great" Britain, he'd been left for dead and even worse, seen his beloved wife left in the same position. Not to mention the people you get to know on the streets and who you really do grow to love. Emotions develop fast in extreme surroundings. I can't really put it into words to you the grief I feel when I walk through Ilford and I see people I know slowly dying. I'm crying for them, I'm crying for me, I'm crying for Mick and Michelle and I can't process any of these things until I've let these things out. But never on the streets. I will find a toilet to sob in, or go down an alley — I know how to express my tears quickly and efficiently. I never wipe them dry. I let them leave salty tracks down my face. That day Mick wept his heart out and we all felt better, like after a thunderstorm.

But recently I've been struggling to find that trigger. Needing to cry and not being able to, I can only describe, is like having wind and not being able to fart or burp. It's agonising. Which is actually quite funny, when you put it like that. Anyway, there are, apparently seven stages of grief. I'm at number four. I did the shock, felt the pain, rather enjoyed the anger (although it is utterly unsustainable) and now I think I'm approaching the sadness/loneliness bit. It's incredibly lonely. Because nobody but your brothers and sisters who have, or are, on the streets, will ever understand that feeling. And you don't want to bore people by talking about it. Especially when they rush to change the subject.

But what AM I grieving for? The world was not what I thought it was and many of its inhabitants are disappointing. That's okay. So can I be. Others, however, are downright evil. Anyway, I've had the scales lifted from my eyes. I see the divinity and I see very clearly the opposite of that, too.

"Tis here where hell and heaven dance" wrote Kate Bush on Constellation of the Heart. Never a truer word. Though Ilford has overdone the hell bit, a bit.

One of the strangest and most divine things that happens to you when you are in real trouble with the darker side, is that someone always comes along and gives you the advice you really need. One night, I was in Wetherspoons, Leytonstone, raging into my phone to Mick and Michelle. I had spent the whole day gathering £30 so I would have enough to get through the next week. I'd walked several miles to get there. Then I put ten pounds in the Underground Oyster machine, It swallowed my money and didn't give me my card. The TFL transport guard saw what had happened and went to investigate the machine. He said there was no record of my payment. I said "Well, you saw me put it in." Will you please investigate this again. He went back, but this time he had locked the keys into the station office. "I'll have to go to Leyton and get another set," he told me. "FFS!," I said under my breath. I went outside to wait the half hour for him to return and starting spilling my woes to this girl sitting out the front begging. She was clearly on heroin, but she was sweet and I gave her some cigarette dog ends. I was only just calming down when a man walked past and shouted "junkie" at her.

I didn't take the time to check out what he looked like. I swiveled like a banshee and roared "fuck you!!" in his face. I literally blew him back about six steps with my voice and rage. Then I looked up and noticed he was a good foot taller than me, with a big scar on his face. "Oh fuck" I thought, and marched off, leaving behind my £10 refund. It wouldn't have been there anyway, I know that.

When I got to Wetherspoons I was trying to calm my nerves by listening to ABBA as I always do, It really wasn't working. And I was pacing. This lovely Portuguese guy came up to me. "What are you listening to?'"he asked. I popped on 'Thank You For the Music' for him and he smiled, patting my shoulder and I instantly felt calmer. "Stay in the light," he told me.

"Stay in the light".

7th | East London | On the Game

Andrew Fraser

Do you ever get the feeling that this country is about to fall apart at the seams? In brighter economic times, this government "invested" in tax cuts for the super rich. 'Cos they, like *really* needed the dough. Meanwhile, I've spent a year trying to get counselling for my trauma, during which time I've been thrown back on the streets because I was not considered to be traumatised enough. How they'd know, is anyone's guess, because I've never been granted an audience with any kind of specialist. They call my condition Post Traumatic Stress Disorder, but, trust me, there is nothing "post" about it.

Calling trauma an illness is like calling a bullet wound an illness. They're not. They are both, just wounds, inflicted by life. Most cogent and awake people are traumatised to some extent. It would be weird not to be, in this world — unless you spend your entire life chained to your mobile phone and zoning out of the reality of existence. Which many do. The pharmaceutical industry, meanwhile, knows very well that it is better and probably cheaper, in the long run, to give trauma survivors talking therapies rather than load them with laboratory created heroin which turns them into zombies. But you've got a better chance of catching a salmon in Manchester Ship canal than getting talking therapies through your GP.

Oh GPs! My shit list is long but these greedy charlatans are right near the top. Asking a GP about anything more complicated than a head cold is like asking the girl in Argos how they made the computer she just sold you. GPs are basically just superannuated shop assistants. They're all on the game. They just use a different name …

I've been trying for the last month to get an appointment with my GP. Even for an appointment a week ahead, you have to call the minute they turn on the phone lines. After days of trying, I finally got through, bang on opening time, last Thursday. I must have been their first caller. I asked for that appointment in a week's time.

"It's a half-day next Thursday, so they've all gone," the receptionist told me. Nice work if you can get it eh?

"But they can't have all gone," I pleaded. "It's 8.46, your lines have been open for one minute". She sighed with exasperation, I was clearly being difficult.

"You will have to try again tomorrow," she told me.

"But I won't get THROUGH tomorrow. You KNOW this!" She was getting irritable now.

"Look, you will have to get off the line now. There are other people trying to get through".

How very selfish of me, I thought. Slapped wrists.

"But what's the point in answering their calls,'" I asked her. "You won't help them either. I KNOW this because I've been trying for weeks".

"Do NOT raise your voice to me!" Oh God.

"Bye!"

She's as elusive as Santa in summer, my GP, but when I do get to meet her she is quite nice. Not like the last one who I asked for counselling from and asked her to renew my medical certificate.

"Get a job!" she spat.

"I could say the same thing to you love," I responded. "You just sit there Googling everything. You hadn't even heard of Seasonal Affective Disorder. I'm gonna lose all my benefits because of you and all you do is try to press Diazepam on me. Are they sponsoring you or summat?"

But the nice one promised I'd get a phone call, urgently, from some medical authority or other to arrange trauma therapy. Two-and-a-half months later I'm still waiting. I was highly distressed at that meeting. I still have horrible night terrors among other symptoms of trauma. She gave me an emergency 24-hour trauma helpline number. One night I needed it and rang it. It rang out for about three minutes then went dead. After the third attempt it went through to a voicemail with a promise that I would be called back. I never was.

Whether you are on the street or off it, you are suffering intense trauma and almost certainly in no fit state to work without outside assistance getting your head and your broken heart back together. Still GPs who know nothing about homelessness or its effects refuse medical certificates to those who have found temporary housing or those still on the streets, because they decide in their infinite wisdom that it's time they pull themselves together. When they refuse your medical certificate you can't pay your rent because they stop your benefits. You are bundled back on the streets to die thanks to the superannuated shop assistants. And the trauma and pain multiplies every time they send you back from whence you came. My friend Yolanda spent many years sleeping rough. She warned me. "They don't care about you. But if you die, there will have to be an inquest and it will come out that they didn't help you when you were in need which might affect their reputation and so their ability to make pots of cash". Once a month, she gets up early, fries an egg ... runny yoke. Then she slaps it on her coat. Other times it's Baked Beans in her hair. "Be careful not to go too far," she said. "You might accidentally get sectioned." So she gets there at quarter to eight and stands in a long queue for her emergency appointment. Then she sits with the yoke on her blouse, rocks gently back and forth and groans: "Doctor, I think I'm walking in the Vale of Darkness..." She gets her certificate and to keep her home for another month. Maybe her words, when it comes to GPs, are truer than she realises.

8th | Brighton | Labour's Grand Design

Circus Street squatters

Construction officially begins on a £130 million scheme converting Brighton's former fruit and veg market into 450 student bedrooms and 142 houses. Of these, 28 will be "affordable" housing — 80% of market rents for eligible households. The average rent for a bedroom in Brighton was £977 per month in August.

This is the new development taking place in the back garden of our old home on Circus Street.

More gentrification, more social cleansing of the working class of our city. Fancy new developments mean bigger profits for businesses and bastard property developers and higher prices and rising rents for everyone else in a city which is already seeing an exodus of working people unable to afford rising rents, and is "home" to a homeless population that has nearly doubled in the last year alone.

Of course, there is no promise of affordable accommodation, but there is the promise of more private student accommodation ripping off students in our city, one of the causes of student homelessness in our city.

What's more, there are claims that the new development will provide space for creative projects. But this fails to acknowledge the fact that most creatives are piss poor and among those people being forced out of our city by developments just like this one. The vast majority of creatives, particularly aspiring creatives trying to carve out their place in the world, don't have money to spend on hiring "creative spaces". Squats and social centres like our DIY social centre, where we gave people the opportunity to use the space for galleries and art exhibitions, for free, are the places that we need for a real artistic community.

This Labour controlled Brighton & Hove City Council promised to eradicate street homelessness by 2020 but as they stall on opening empty buildings and throw resources at ejecting homeless workers and students from
empty buildings, whilst facilitating property development projects such as
this, it is clear that ex-copper Warren Morgan and the rest of his Labour
council are on the side of the gentrifiers, not the working people of this city.

11th | East London | A Walk in the Park

Andrew Fraser

Being homeless is like being a refugee in your own land. Refugees have
camps. Why do homeless people not have homeless camps? We are, after
all, internal refugees. Refugees from years of government greed and
neglect of the housing crisis in our country, neglect of mental health
services, neglect of simple, decent human standards of behaviour that
should say that your fellow man or woman is your brother or sister.
Not somebody left out in the rain to die. Refugees from greed. Now the
chickens are all coming home to roost and it ain't pretty. It's gonna get
far, far uglier …

There is, of course, a reason why there are no homeless camps in
London. There is a reason why we cannot take our tents to Valentine's
Park and pitch up there at night, away from the casual violence of the
streets. It is foolhardy to sleep there alone, but if all the homeless people
of Ilford went to sleep there together, tonight, they would be out of the
hair of Marks and Spencer, not making the place look untidy. And they
could look out for one another.

So why do the police harass and threaten people who sleep there, con-
fiscating and ripping up their tents?

Big problems deserve big solutions. Would it not make sense to requisition a public park in London or Manchester or any of our big cities and hand it over to our homeless brothers and sisters. Charities could provide portaloos, showers. Groups that care for homeless people would know where to find them, as they wouldn't be scattered all over their cities. Food could be brought by people who care. Tents could be provided. In the winter, extra blankets, hot water bottles. It is a simple and logical short term solution.

But there is a reason why homeless people are not allowed to gather and sleep in our public parks (even though ridiculous 1980s revivalist festivals are allowed to set up shop there over a number of days, as are circuses and fairgrounds). If even one London park was to declare itself a safe zone for homeless people, then they would all gather there. Then we would finally see the scale of the humanitarian disaster facing our country and our cities. People would be, rightly, horrified. The numbers of homeless people exceed the estimated numbers by a country mile. And in one great big ugly, smelly, blot on the landscape, our nation would finally get to see for itself what it has done to those most desperately in need of help.

That's why it's police policy to scatter homeless people far and wide. Unfortunately the problem is becoming too big now. There are too many of us. Even if you scatter us, we are popping up everywhere. What are they to do? Certainly, there are more and more of us dying — especially given the prevalence of Spice, smack and crack on the streets. That suits the authorities and the police certainly aren't doing much to stop this trade, which is taking place right under their noses. As I've said before, it's a kind of slow genocide. But it's not happening fast enough.

The number of people becoming homeless is rapidly exceeding the number of people dying from the effects of homelessness. The authorities have got a real problem on their hands. We have a humanitarian crisis on our hands, and as much as we, as individuals can and should help out — it will take government action to really make a change. It seems fairly simple how to start to make things better.

- Build homes.
- End the vicious outdated vagrancy laws which make it a crime to ask for help.
- Make our green city spaces a place of refuge and safety for home-less people.

Marks and Spencer finally got in touch with me today. Let's give them a chance. Perhaps they can help us pressure Redbridge Council into giving up some public land for homeless people to sleep safely in, seeing as there are no beds in night shelters anymore.

• • •

It's funny how homelessness affects your view on everything. When you have been in that situation it will haunt you for the rest of your life.

I used to love the sound of rain when I was indoors and didn't need to go out. Now, if I'm lucky enough to have a roof over my head at the time, I lie there listening to it, feeling sick with guilt about my friends who are still out there in it.

I used to love London and my country. I genuinely never believed I could possibly fall out of love with it. I loved its cultural diversity, the sense of adventure that comes from never really knowing what's going to happen next, the feeling of boundless possibility.

But now all I see are the joins. I used to love the ungentrified parts, they felt "real", raw, genuine. But on a trip around Newham last week, all I could see was the grinding poverty. Yes, it's great, you can pick up a samosa for 50p. Those things used to excite me. I love a bargain after all. But what if you haven't got 50p? Now all I see is a return to the days of Dickens and there is nothing worth romanticising about that. The posh bits, which are meant to impress us, are even more depressing because I know that wealth has been created mostly by property speculators not caring that their actions have left so many people to suffer. "I'm alright jack." It's piss elegant, as they say up north.

For me, the party is over, and I pray for the day I get to leave this city and this country for somewhere civilised. I yearn for Greece or for Georgia in the Caucasus, where you are treated like a guest in some-one's home. Nobody has much in these ancient countries, but everybody shares.

And yeah, I will always prefer a rough east end boozer to one that's been dollied up and made presentable. To somewhere which stinks of money but has no class, somewhere which, as my granny would have ob-served correctly, is all fur coat and no knickers. Sums up London really. Now I know why they call them the "filthy rich".

17th | East London | Misfit

Andrew Fraser

I probably shouldn't say it, but sometimes homelessness is quite fun. Well it was for me anyway. Terrible huh?

But y'know, of *course* I didn't choose it or want it, of course it was horrible and traumatising. Of course you wouldn't wish it on your worst enemy. But my spirit knew it couldn't afford to collapse into despair and self-pity. You cannot afford to be depressed on the streets. Anxious — of course, hyper-vigilant, naturally — but depression? No, that comes afterwards, when you realise how little the world values your life — but at the time you are in the midst of it, the adrenalin starts to kick in. The old flight or fight reflex. Once you have quickly caught up with the fact that this is your life now … and you might not have very long left, it's kinda liberating, kinda exciting.

And no matter what the rest of the world thinks of you, you feel proud, you actually feel strong. I had spent my life being afraid of my own shadow, on too many occasions. But with homelessness, I rose to the occasion. I am good at being homeless. I took to it like a duck to water. I have resources I was not aware of; sharp instincts and a quick brain. I understand the value of respect, and that's very important on the streets. You can be the hardest fucker in London, but if you are arrogant, self-serving and, generally, a wanker — you will last weeks before someone "deals" with you. Spiritually, intellectually and physically, I found out that I was quick on my feet. You have to be.

I'd spent all my life feeling like an outsider, from being a Geordie to being gay, I never fitted in anywhere. I lasted one week in the Cub Scouts before, much to my father's fury, I refused to go back. I refused to play their games or follow their rules. "If I want to make a fire with sticks, I'll make a fire with sticks but I'm not doing it just because the rest of you are," I remember thinking, at six years old. "I'd rather read my comics" In large groups I'd always find the seat nearest the door. I'd feel short of breath whenever I was dragged into being "part" of some kind of gang or scene.

I remember this idiot once telling me I wasn't a 'team player' because I left a group I was on holiday with, to go off for a wander on my own. I felt very relieved by his observation. I didn't relate to my home town, I hated huge swathes of the media when I was part of it and I feel no affinity to gay men just because we might desire the same folk. I have always been an awkward bastard. A square peg in a round hole.

There was always a deep sense of feeling rejected by the world. But really, it was always me doing the rejecting. It's not that I thought I was any better than them. Well, not most. I just didn't see why I should be browbeaten into having an affinity with someone just because their first language was the same as mine or some other spurious notion of identity.

But as a homeless man, I fitted in instinctively. Down among the rejects. I knew instinctively how to be. That first night down at Stratford Shopping Centre, I knew exactly what to do. I popped to the off-licence on the way and bought six cans of Tyskie, then shoulders back, head high I strolled calmly and patiently through to a spot where I felt it would be safe to park up my sleeping back. I felt oddly serene but I also knew, never, ever show fear. I handed out a couple of cans to a pair of funny, loveable Romanian ne'er do wells who looked like a laugh and asked them if they would mind if I slept down near to them. They cleared me a spot and I knew instantly they had my back. Adrenaline was pumping through me, previously I had been in that disgusting hostel in Leytonstone, among the crackheads and smackheads who robbed and threatened to stab me. I knew I was okay among a few common or garden alcoholics.

And we had a laugh, sitting up pretty much all of the night, singing while my Romanian friend Ion strummed his guitar. I'd recently taken to singing up at Newbury Park Station so it was nice to have bandmates, as he roared "WE WILL WE WILL RACK YOU!" Queen are big amongst Romanian homeless men. It was nice to be around sweetness, having just experienced such viciousness — I had been in danger of losing my life on four of the last five nights, and I don't know if it was the euphoria of knowing that I'd somehow survived, or just their hilarious company, which made me think at one point, "this is the best night out of my life!"

Maybe it was. I certainly felt free. I had nothing left to lose apart from my life and I was no longer scared about that happening, having found my connection to God. I spent the early hours chilling with a lovely elderly rapper from Jamaica, who was also a comedian and we opened a few more beers. If we closed our eyes we could have been looking at Montego Bay and not Poundland. I had talked to many that night. Most were, like myself, artists of one kind or another. I'd been noticing that a lot. There are not a lot of homeless PR people, accountants or HR executives. I reckon about 85% of the rest though are singers, writers, painters, comedians, poets, chefs … And the remaining 15% probably should be …

It was the same thought that struck me in Waltham Forest Housing, seeing all these lives being destroyed by something which was not parsimony but vindictiveness. I was speaking to the other people in the queues … almost without fail, creative people. This world does not value art nor respect artists. It's all about the moolah. And if you do make it, the money that you generate will usually end up in the hands of the people without an artistic bone in their bodies. Parasites. I recalled how the first thing the Nazis did, when they came to power, was to destroy art. And I watched as this government and society destroyed these people's lives and quietened their voices.

Anyway. having danced and sung up a storm with my Jamaican and Romanian fellow misfits down Stratford station, I fell asleep around 4.30am with a smile on my face for the first time in weeks. I awoke to a prodding in my right soldier. I looked up and this enormously rotund woman was bearing down on me.

"Do you need help?" she asked. "I've never seen you before. Who are you?"

"Who are YOU?' I asked? 'Do YOU need help?" I asked, returning the compliment. I had had my fill of interfering fake do-gooders on fine salaries.

"I'm from Thames Reach Charity and I've come to help you," she said smiling sweetly.

"Oh, so you work for the government deporting East Europeans against their will," I told her. "You grass them up, right?"

"No we don't'" she said.

"Well I happen to know for a fact that you do,' I told her. So you are not only a grass but a liar". I leapt out of my sleeping bag.

"No I'm not. No we're not," she said.

"Liar, liar, Bum's on fire!" I yelled in her face. "You and 'Saint' Mungo's do it. Incidentally, it was your mates at 'Saint Mungo's that nearly got me killed three times over three days after I blogged about your insidious activities".

"No we don't," she lied, strolling off to patronise a young disabled girl. I barged in.

"What have they ever done for you?" I asked the girl, blocking the fat woman's path.

"Nothing," said the girl. "They come here for weeks on end, but all they do is ask questions, they never actually do anything". I turned to look at the woman from Thames Reach.

"Other charities come with food, toiletries, real help…what do you actually DO?" I demanded.

"Will you PLEASE get out of my way and stop obstructing my work".

"No," I roared back."'I want explanations. What do you actually fucking do apart from grass people up and gather information. And get people deported against their will? If you wanna help why don't you just go out and buy us all a burger instead of standing there with your head tilted pretending that you care. Let's face it, you've had more than your own fair share of burgers by the looks of things. I bet you're getting a great salary to pay for all that grub. I bet your job sounds great at dinner parties, don't it? Telling everyone you work for a charity when in fact you're the fifth column".

She looked angry but her eyes wouldn't meet my own.

"We don't do that". she said, finally raising her voice. There was a big crowd gathering around us now. All homeless, I could hear them saying, words to the effect of, "They've never done anything for us".

This young Polish guy burst through the crowd. "Yes you do," he yelled. "You got my best mate deported after he gave you his details".

I jumped for joy. "There you go, you fucking lying cow. Now fuck off out of here and leave these people alone. Seriously. fuck off". The crowd began to laugh and clap and they sensibly departed. Never trust Saint Mungo's or Thames Reach and NEVER give to them. Evil bastards who pretend to care about the vulnerable in society while making a good living out of their predicaments and simultaneously stitching them up.

I'd had the night of my life and I got the tube back to a Sikh temple with my Jamaican rapper mate, who had me in stitches the whole way, as we rode the underground. I looked around at how miserable everybody else on train looked, how frightened so many of their faces were. Presumably scared of losing the rat race and ending up where we were. But you know, in the moment I KNEW I was happier than they were. And I really did feel free of the matrix. And the moment is, really all we ever have.

20th | Manchester | Burnham's Raid

Freedom News

Homeless people rounded on Andy Burnham's Labour administration in Manchester today after 20 people were rousted out of the well-regarded Cornerhouse squatted centre in an early-morning raid.

Manchester Activist Network, which has been heavily involved in the space, said today they will be looking to hold highly-paid council bosses to account for promises made during Mayor Burnham's election campaign in May that his team would "end rough sleeping by 2020":

"Well done Andy Burnham and Manchester Council. Help end rough sleeping by 2020? Don't you mean make 20 more people street homeless? Where's the promises now eh? Spineless".

The dynamic entry assault came out of the blue as members of the self-organised homeless squat and social centre were planning the first screenings of a documentary on the outstanding grassroots work which has been done by Cornerhouse and the Manchester Activist Network this year.

Established in a former arts centre that had been empty for the previous two years, which is owned by Network Rail, Cornerhouse was one of the most successful self-organised street homeless projects of recent years, providing both housing and a community arts space for most of 2017.

At its height,the organising group was able to coordinate with a second larger residential squat, Hotspur Press, which was itself evicted last month — meaning that in the first three months of the new administration taking power pledging to end Manchester's street homeless crisis around 60 people have been pushed back into street homelessness.

Squatters were highly sceptical of headlines from Burnham about "putting promises into action" over reducing homelessness when he took power on May 8th this year, but had made an effort to engage with his agenda, suggesting that he come and visit Cornerhouse to hear direct from people at the sharp end about what's actually needed.

Burnham never made it down to the centre, just round the corner from Oxford Road Station, and has so far failed to respond to either eviction, though he had plenty of time on August 1st to wander around Manchester city centre and put out a vague charity appeal to "end rough sleeping by 2020". Talking to *Freedom News*, MAN organisers David Blaine and Nick Napier said:

"We're sitting down with our family from the Cornerhouse after our rude awakening this morning, 20 people with whom we are now once again street homeless and pondering, what do we do now?

"'I pledge to end rough sleeping by 2020,' that was your promise to the people of Manchester Andy Burnham. That number seems to be very relevant today, 20 more people on the street sleeping rough, 20 more victims, 20 more statistics, 20 more possible deaths on your hands caused by your empty promises.

"You won an election on the back of victims like those evicted today and who you failed to support. For seven months the Cornerhouse was a safe haven for those neglected by you and your council, after several face-to-face meetings, at the Cornerhouse, your hustings, your events on housing, your Q&As, your national news articles, your glossy photo opportunities, you know the truth, you know our situation, you said that you understood and you said that you cared.

"Your colleagues Paul Dennett, Beth Knowles and Ivan Lewis MP all knew the truth and wanted to come and see the community that we had built. You wanted to witness the truth. Where were you Andy? Where was your support? Your words and promises are empty. Empty just like the buildings that we occupy, just like the buildings YOU asked for! It was less than £30 to lease our building, your mayoral fund was set up for this.

"It's time to stop the BS Andy, no more messing around. The next building we take and those we support in it will require your help Andy Burnham, no more passing the buck, no more UK evictions, no more court cases. #housingisahumanright, #housingfirst and for this we will stand and make a fight, #nomoredeathsonourstreets".

22nd | Brighton | Pride and Prejudices

Homeless Pride Brighton

What an amazing day we had at Homeless Pride Brighton on Sunday. We were so happy to see so many of the community enjoying activities ranging from weaving to Scrufts dog show, from a chat with chai tea to giant Jenga, and of course the great selection of music from local acts and buskers.

We achieved our aim of a celebration of the lives of the homeless, whether they be on the street, part of the invisible homeless community or those who are living precariously close to homelessness. As a team made up mostly of people who have experienced or are experiencing homelessness, this was a personal celebration. But there were also people who had their awareness around these issues raised, and through the activities met with people they may never have before.

As this was the first event, there were of course a couple of hiccups. We extend our apologies to the local business whose toilets were overrun, and to those who were affected by the bass of the DJ set. We finished at 8pm to avoid evening disturbance and regularly read a sound meter and had hoped this would be effective. In future, these things would be ironed out.

30th | East London | Educated Criminals Work Within the Law

Andrew Fraser

I wouldn't exactly call street mugging a noble art, but there's certainly a refreshing honesty to it. They wave the knife at your throat, you hand over the dough, they run off. I know, it's happened to me too many times on the streets and before. It's not great but at least they're not like mobile phone companies. You know where you stand with muggers and it's worth the tenner you lost to not have to spend hours on end fruitlessly negotiating with them in call centres in far off lands only to be routinely lied to, cut off and then left with the dawning realisation that you've signed a contract, they've got you by the balls and now they have your money they're gonna make it as difficult as possible for you to escape their clutches or get your money back, however shitty their product is.

I once spent nearly six hours on the phone to a Virgin Call Centre, being cut off repeatedly, demanding that they fix the crappy phone they sent me which they broke through a faulty download, only to be told by the bloke on the end of the phone: "Well I've worked for Vodafone and T-Mobile and they're much worse".

But it's not just mobile phone companies. Banks, GPs, lawyers, estate agents, basically anyone who sells anything over the phone or on the street, charity muggers … we live in a "take the money and run" society. Let's not forget politicians. And watching them all with their snouts in the trough, you think: "Well, if they can do it and get away with it why shouldn't I?" So some kid who tries to copy these "respectable" role models and nicks a load of trainers from JD Sports ends up being fed drugs behind bars while they waltz away with their crimes. Because he didn't know the golden rule. If you are gonna steal, just know the law and pirouette around the outlines of it, without ever crossing over that line. Meanwhile some nasty-arsed businessman can put his company into liquidation, leaving hundreds of hard working people unpaid, waltz away and then set up the same venture a few weeks later untouched by justice. These people have blood on their hands.

It happens in the public sector too. My friend Jimmy just got into a place after more than a year on the streets. He gets fuck all in benefits but still has to fork out for council tax. He got a bill two months ago telling him he needed to hurry up and pay around £20 a month. He's suffering from PTSD like me and he's very anxious and disordered and he genuinely forgot. Anyway a few days ago he got a terrifying letter in bold, blood-red ink from Barking and Dagenham council tax services. He had three days to pay the entire bill for the year (which of course he couldn't do) or they were adding £190 to his bill (for what?) taking him to court (costs money!) and sending the bailiffs around. Luckily for Jimmy he's got fuck all to confiscate. But that exercise will also presumably cost money.

Jimmy tried to call them over several days, to offer to pay some of what little he has left, so they might call the legal dogs off. It took 35 minutes first time and it's not Vodafone so he ran out of credit after 27 minutes. The next day he spent money topping up his phone and tried again but again the waiting time was over half an hour and he didn't have enough money to both pay the call and pay their bill. Eventually he walked three miles to their offices in Dagenham assuming he would be able to pay. It's called the "one stop shop" so it's meant to deal with everything council related, but apparently it's everything bar council tax. They let him use their phone to call through to the single human being dealing with council tax enquiries (who works in the same building!) but the waiting time was again half an hour and he missed the cut before the phone lines close at 5pm. He will no doubt try again tomorrow.

Had they bothered to look into his health records, which they do have, they would have discovered that Jimmy was very nearly sectioned on many occasions recently for feeling suicidal. By tomorrow he will be a day late so they will have no doubt by then applied the £190 "fine" to his bill. Well, you can't get blood out of a stone so it's a futile exercise doing that to a man who doesn't even own cutlery. But, like the dishonourable people mentioned above, by the time this is sorted out, they might well yet have actual blood on their hands. It won't say that on his death certificate though. It will say "misadventure".

30th | Glasgow | What's Your Bid?

Freedom News

A Freedom of Information request from Homeless Scotland has turned up a phenomenon of rough sleepers being pushed into doing Housing Options assessments by Glasgow City Council — meaning that those in greatest need are being asked to "bid" for a home and then wait up to seven months for help rather than being offered adequate immediate assistance.

Homeless Scotland explains:

"I want you to picture the scene...

"For months you have been rough sleeping, sofa-surfing, or staying in some form of unsuitable accommodation, and you finally pluck up the courage to present as homeless to Glasgow City Council.

"Say, for example, you cannot face sleeping on the streets anymore, and you visit the casework team, hopeful that you'll be offered accommodation — as you know the council have a legal duty to provide you with temporary accommodation while they assess your case, so you go there confident that they will fulfil their statutory duties.

"Imagine you visited the council, and the caseworker tells you they will complete a Housing Options application form with you. They inform you that you need to 'bid' for properties online, and that you will eventually be offered your own property.

"Surely not! Surely my sources got confused — anyone in a homeless situation would be told that a full homeless application would be completed and they would be provided with accommodation in the meantime.

"Unfortunately, it would appear that my sources are spot on …"

The FoI request showed that, rather than being placed in temporary accommodation while having their case dealt with, of the 9,720 Housing Options applications carried out last year, the following were told to fill out Housing Options forms but not offered immediate assistance:

- 75 rough sleepers ("long term roofless")
- 67 long-term sofa surfers
- 885 people who were homeless following a stint in prison
- 80 people released from hospital who were homeless

Meaning well over one in ten of the applications were being made by people who should have been treated as priority cases for immediate assistance, but weren't. Homeless Scotland continued:

"On what planet is it acceptable for rough sleepers not to be given a full homeless application? I could not believe what I was reading today.

"The average length of stay in temporary accommodation was given as 81 days, and includes all types of temporary accommodation (B&Bs, hostels, supported accommodation). The average length of time someone waits before being offered their own mainstream accommodation using Housing Options is given as 194 days.

"So if people are in temporary accommodation for an average of 81 days, and are waiting 194 for their own tenancy, where the hell are they going for the missing 113 days? Seven months of waiting for people who should have been offered homeless accommodation there and then?

"Housing Options is fine if you are staying somewhere safe and secure, and are in no rush for your own flat. If you can wait roughly 194 days, then there's no issue. But when a huge proportion of the people are presenting to the council when they are homeless, and are getting fobbed off with a Housing Options application instead of a full homeless application, then there is something still seriously wrong with the system.

"With all the people dying on the streets when sleeping rough making headlines in the press in Glasgow over the last few months, I'd love to know how many of these poor souls approached Glasgow City Council for help … and only completed a Housing Options application. 'Yes sir, you'll be fine sleeping on the streets for the next 194 days, what's the worst that could happen?' In May this year, the newspapers told us that 39 homeless people died on the streets in the space of 10 months.

"So let me summarise this, let me clarify the situation, just in case I'm not being clear here. In Glasgow, 75 rough sleepers who presented as homeless to Glasgow City Council, completed an application for mainstream tenancies, instead of full homelessness applications, and were sent on their way.

"The press told us in May that four people were dying every month on the streets. So, on average, just over six rough sleepers presented for assistance to Glasgow City Council every month during the year from April 2016 to the end of March 2017, and were sent back to where they came from after completing a Housing Options application where the average waiting time for a tenancy is seven months.

"Roughly four people rough sleeping are dying on the streets every month. And six people who are rough sleeping present to the council as homeless every month are getting sent on their way by Glasgow City Council, after completing an application designed for folk who have time on their hands. And yet Glasgow City Council responded to these deaths in the press by saying that it was the "life-style" of the rough sleepers that was to blame for all those deaths.

"I disagree. Perhaps if those 75 rough sleepers were given the type of service they were entitled to when presenting as homeless to Glasgow City Council, a large proportion of those deaths could have been prevented. But that's not much consolation for the friends, families and loved ones of the folk that died though, is it? And yet still no one will be held to account!"

SEPTEMBER

A National Audit Office report on homelessness summarises: "Homelessness in all its forms has significantly increased in recent years, driven by several factors. Despite this, government has not evaluated the impact of its reforms on this issue, and there remain gaps in its approach. It is difficult to understand why the Department persisted with its light touch approach in the face of such a visibly growing problem. Its recent performance in reducing homelessness therefore cannot be considered value for money". No evaluation has been made of the impact of austerity since its introduction in the early 2010s, the NAO notes, but spending on temporary accomodation is now £845 million.

1st | East London | Brooke House

Andrew Fraser

Context: Working with BBC Panorama, a whistleblower exposed horrific treatment of detainees in overcrowded centres designed to hold people for only short periods, but which ended up overcrowded with long-term cases. The probe into Brook House, run by G4s, showed widespread self-harm, attempted suicides, endemic drug use and high levels of violence as people struggled to deal with being detained indefinitely while they awaited processing in the courts for their asylum cases.

I told you that fake charities Saint Mungo's and Thames Reach grass homeless foreigners up who are then rounded up and deported against their will. Well THIS is where my brothers and sisters off the streets end up. Now that's just the first part of this horrific story once these people are stripped of all human rights they are stuck on a plane and 'sent back'. Does anyone know where? Does anyone care what happens to them on the other side? I've heard people say "well maybe they'd be better off with their families" ... well, I very much doubt there's a taxi waiting to sweep them back to mama on the other side. Things must be deadly bad if they prefer life on the streets here cos it is hideous. God bless this whistleblower guy. Hope his life is safe because they don't want you to know this shit.

5th | East London | But for the Grace of God

Andrew Fraser

Welcome to the McCreadie hotel in Forest Gate, London. Otherwise known as the Hammered House of Horrors.

It is set in no obvious acres of parkland in an area of London you really don't wish to go to which has oddly been christened Forest Gate. The Forest is long gone and if there is a gate it needs to be locked, permanently. To say Forest Gate is a shithole is to do a massive disservice to shitholes the world over. So apologies to Middlesbroughs and downtown Cincinnati. This place is the real deal and, to be fair, the only logical, spiritual home for the McCreadie Hotel.

It wasn't always thus. Once upon a time Forest Gate was a standard bearer for multicultural London. It was the kind of place I loved to hang out in. A bit fucked up but with every kind of community there. All rubbing along. What London is all about, or so I thought.

Then came Brexit, inflicted on us by people from Cornwall, Wales and Sunderland. And even though it resolutely voted against it, things changed overnight in the capital. There were hidden forces just waiting to be unleashed …

When I was holed up in Forest Gate, at the McGreedy, on my first night mice ate through my phone charger. Seriously. I used to hear them running around the bed and squeaking and although I was knackered, I seriously doubted if I was better off there or outdoors. The sounds of couples fighting violently as they came down from whatever drug they were on, echoed around the halls. I think on my second day, I'd had enough. Half dead but just about able to stand I got to my feet and staggered to the room two doors away where this couple were screaming merry hell at each other. I knocked quietly at the door and then whispered in his face.

"Shut the fuck up and shut your girlfriend up too. I am tired of hearing your disturbing noises. If you don't shut up I swear I'll do it for you. Go and yell at each other in the street". He saw that I was near demented with tiredness and wisely, they went out to yell at each other in the street, as suggested.

When I picked myself up, I found a local takeaway owned by a lovely Persian man. He told me how Brexit had changed everything. Just a week earlier two feral Polish guys dragged a young muslim lad out from the takeaway into the street to give him a beating for no other reason than his religion. He jumped in and stopped it. Weeks earlier, a group of Muslim lads decided to knock seven bells out of a white lad, same bullshit reason.

"Where did all this hatred come from?" I asked him. "I don't recognise my city anymore". He shook his head sadly.

"It was always there. These people were just looking for an excuse and Brexit gave it to them".

Anyway, weeks after I got made homeless for the third time there was someone kind enough to put me in the McCreadie hotel for a week. I didn't realise how tired I was. Your body does a weird thing when your life is in danger. It keeps pumping out adrenaline. So there I was. In an actual room. With a roof and a door. And a lock. And when I got there I dissolved. Honestly once that door was locked I dissolved. When I finally woke up. I think it was two days later. Didn't know where the fuck I was. Managed to find the local Wetherspoons though. I can always do that. I liked it there. Even though its rough in Forest Gate those people took to me. There is a community of feral cats living at the pub and I saw myself.

I had the room for a few more nights. But I had no money. So I would walk or hike to Newbury Park station, to make a few bob. But I became Ill. A year on and off the streets, I'd never been Ill. I still never get Ill.

But this time I was. I would be out all day, right as rain, but as soon as I got back to my room in the McCready, I started to retch into the bin. I lost my voice completely which made it hard for me to shout at wankers but more importantly to sing. Singing saved my life.

I saw my mate Carl in Ilford and whispered to him that I was in the McCready and I had no voice. He rolled his eyes. "It's because you're inhaling the crack smoke" he said. He was right. People on crack and smack get housed, before people who don't. I used to see them rocking from side to side and I resented them. Forgive me but I did.

Anyway I managed to get out of that hellhole and into somewhere else. A lot of my friends are now smoking Spice. You don't even want to know what that does to a human brain or heart. I'm okay. By the skin of my teeth. There but for the grace of God.

8th | Manchester | Lessons of Cornerhouse

Nick Napier of Manchester Activist Network, in Freedom Journal

As the final pieces of our belongings, donations and clothes were brought out of the infamous Cornerhouse it was time for Manchester Activist Network to reflect back on six months of occupation. From the Loose Space festival and surviving three eviction attempts, to the rough sleepers we housed and three other squats opened over that time, this had been a busy, and at times stressful but productive period that none of us will ever forget.

The biggest thing that came out of the Cornerhouse was a reaffirmation of the need for solidarity when we are faced with big issues. In order to fully tackle rough sleeping and stop the rise in homelessness we all need to be prepared to give a little of ourselves. Not money, but from inside of us. We need constructive dialogues, we need to drop the egos, forget about the "company line," reflect on what we put our energies into and how we can change as individuals. Only then can we better the systemic problem that is homelessness.

Our experience of the Cornerhouse starts with Loose Space, a five-week festival we held. It was a double-edged sword. It did exactly what we hoped it would; bring artists and the community together with activists, and enable a sharing of ideologies and effort. However this came at a cost to many of us personally as it tested our bonds of friendship and ideology, and was physically and mentally draining. I think we would all agree though that it had more positives than negatives.

We are still here solid as a group, at time of writing have three squats and have brought in new faces who have given additional energy in areas we did not have access to before, like film, social media, arts/crafts, healing, contact through the MMU and fundraising for three worthy charities. All of these were goals before the festival, so in my eyes it was a great success.

It has taught us a lot more about squatting, particularly when you have a group of around 40 people. There is a need for different types of squats: Residential, Activist, Arts and Healing are all very different places to live in, however they are essential for any group who wish to be active and create intentional communities to allow the various mix of people, personalities and energy to have the space in which to flourish and be productive to the whole.

Homelessness will never end. We are not the people to end it and no-one should look to us in that way, however, there is a need for us in this city right now. There are many who publicly don't endorse us, yet behind close doors recognise that we provide a service that is lacking at the moment across the UK, not just Manchester. We can as a city end rough sleeping though and this is what we put our energy into at the Cornerhouse.

It is not easy. Dealing with issues that are the causes of homelessness range from drug Vodafone, alcoholism, abuse, youth homelessness, mental illness and the disabled; the list goes on, it is very draining on those individuals that take on mentoring roles, and for people around them as they try to rebuild their lives. We firmly believe now, more than ever, what we did at the Cornerhouse was the right thing to do, and we will continue to do this. Our community of squats grows, and will resolutely put pressure on the council and the associated bodies in Manchester by taking high-profile council buildings and iconic structures in Manchester. Just as rough sleeping doesn't stop overnight, neither will we.

Council failures

Finally, one part of the experience has left a bitter taste in the mouth for many of us. Dealing with politicians. We had a running dialogue with Andrew Lightfoot (CEO, Combined Authority), Mike Wright (Strategic Lead for Homelessness, Combined Authority) Paul Dennett (Mayor of Salford) Beth Knowles (Lead to ending rough sleeping, Labour Council), Ivan Lewis MP, and finally Andrew Burnham (Gtr Manchester Mayor). We had been told that meetings were being arranged with the Mayor and his team, that Beth, Ivan and Paul were coming to visit the squat to see what we did.

We attended the meetings, stayed calm, talked passionately but articulately and tried to engage the people with the power. Where did this leave us? With a broken promise that we would be told the week of eviction to enable us to get some of the more vulnerable members to a new squat, so they were not left to walk the street. That we would be granted a private meeting with Mayor Burnham, and an ignored request from us to postpone any eviction until we had the meetings to give us the best chance to prepare our arguments and points of view.

For me the trust will never be rebuilt and this is the same for many of us, personally it will change the way in which I organise around issues for the remainder of my life.

To wrap things up, the last six months have been a whirlwind of situations, people, buildings, friends, new ideologies and much to ponder. We must however not let our personal stories take the limelight. This is about ALL of us. You, me, the rough sleeper, the abused child, the struggling mum, the mentally ill, to the lonely migrant. This is not just about homelessness either, it is about helping people learn that the time has come for a new paradigm. The old one has run its course, capitalism only fully works for the haves, not the have nots. It only serves a small proportion of the global population and not the many. So now is the time for us to put aside our individual activism issues, come together as one and make change happen. This is the only campaign and it goes on, we only hope that you will start with us today.

10th | East London | Cosy

Andrew Fraser

So I'm at Gants Hill Station. Warm and dry loads of space to sleep. It's pissing it down outside. My mate and her boyfriend actually look quite cosy. Or as cosy as you can sleeping rough. They can't drift into sleep though. If the police catch them they will me "moved on" … to WHERE? They are safe and warm. Why can't they be left alone. Aren't there terrorists to catch? It's all a lie. The police are deployed to attack the poor.

11th | East London | I Wrote Another Book Once

Andrew Fraser

I used to be very trusting before all this, you know. And then, last summer, just before I ended up on the streets for the first time, I finished my first published book. It was my pride and joy. Maybe pride came before a fall. I dunno.

These things seem to happen to me. The day before I got made homeless for the second time, I had performed stand-up comedy down in Vauxhall for the first time. Like most things in my life, it happened by accident. I'd gone into a coffee shop where they were selling my book, to ask if they'd sold any that week. They hadn't. Drat. But there was a nice man in there called Tim who was looking for someone to be the centrepiece of their improvisational comedy night. How could I say no? It was serendipity.

And I did well, even though I do say so myself. It was a buzz and I sold loads of copies, mostly to Americans who I think were glad to come across someone who told them how Europe was just as fucked up as their own country. I felt proud of my book and proud of myself for doing something which was so far out of my comfort zone. It wasn't an ego pride. I'd tapped into something universal which seemed to be giving me the words I needed. I felt honoured to be conferred with the duty of passing on an important message. As I do now. Four nights later I was in casualty on a drip. Five nights later I was kipping on the floor of Stratford shopping centre. Never a dull moment, hey?

And it's hard writing this. For three reasons. One; because I'm sitting in Ilford library shouting at people as kids run and scream around me. A man shouts loudly down his phone which rings every two minutes and they seem to have adopted a "no silence" policy. It's ridiculous and

I'm losing my temper. It's never very far from being lost and, y'know, at least it seems to motivate me to do stuff. But this rude and disrespectful society which we seem to have landed in, seems to be crushing my spirit. I've taken enough for a lifetime. There is no peace.

Secondly, in writing this, I am reliving things which are probably best off forgotten. They say, get it all out on paper (or computer). Well, it would be a waste of an experience not to. Especially when it might help another human being. But sometimes it knocks me for six just to recall what I've lived through.

Thirdly, this is my *Diary of a Rough Sleeper* but it's actually about so much more than that or politics, but take from it what you will. There is stuff I want to say, which I will probably get around to, but it will lose a lot of people, I know. Because I talk about the spiritual side of life, about the things we cannot know and are not able to understand. Over the last year I have witnessed divinity and its opposite. Like I say, never a dull moment. It doesn't happen to everybody, clearly. But it happened to me and it was somehow connected to me writing that book where I spoke about Nazis, the Vatican, dark destructive forces among us. My book wasn't meant to be about that, it was meant to be about how to get cheap flights, but when I travelled to Europe I saw the lessons of history thrown up in the thirties and forties and felt compelled like never before to write about it. I realised how, in British schools, we are taught a lie about our past. If you're not honest about what has gone before you are doomed to repeat it. Little did I know, upon my return, that those forces came roaring back in Europe and North America.

Again, I shouldn't really speak about Brexit because it is not the remit of this blog, But remit-Schmemit. I don't have all the answers but I do know I flew back to a changed city after Brexit where people felt able to say what had been unsayable (because it was plain wrong) or "political correctness" as the *Daily Mail* would have you believe.

As a homeless man, I guess, logically I should be pro-Brexit, right? Errrm, well no. Firstly, because I don't differentiate between people according to where they are born. I am that citizen of the world who Theresa May cursed and said was a "citizen of nowhere" at the Tory Party conference. Maybe she was correct about the latter. I certainly struggle to identify with this country now, after it left me for dead.

But logically, I should be pro-Brexit. Less foreigners mean more homes, right? Well, no actually. First of all, "benefits tourism" is a lie. My homeless friends from Eastern Europe don't get benefits, that's why they are out there dying. Secondly, people are homeless because we have no homes. So what do we need? Money to build affordable homes AND (wait for it...) builders! Chucking out "low-skilled" east European labourers is NOT going to solve the biggest post-war problem this country has ever faced. The housing crisis. We need them.

Thirdly, this whole problem was caused by Tory greed. Contrary to popular belief, the influx of East Europeans and others, skilled or otherwise, was potentially good for this country. They were predominantly young, they didn't sit on their arses collecting benefits, and they paid taxes.

So the economy got a shot in the arm. These enthusiastic young workers helped pay the pensions we could never have afforded, through their contributions to the state. And there was even money left over. But when you add several million people to your population, what you need is to invest the takings in infrastructure. There should have been tens of thousands more homes built, transport improved, schools, spending on health services.

This all could have been done. But did they? Did they heck. They used the windfall to lob 5% off the top rate of income tax. And now the very people who came here and paid for the tax cuts for the very rich are being blamed for the problem. It's never the rich to blame, is it?

Maybe they should go back, I don't know. I certainly would if I had another passport. The working class of this country, of whatever background, has been screwed over and I wish I had somewhere else to go. But blaming them is a red herring. They were sold a lie and now their kids get abused in school and told to "go home" by racist parents, many of home are from immigrant backgrounds themselves. And you know, one fifth of fighters against the Nazis in the Second World War Battle of Britain were from Poland, so a little more respect and historical awareness wouldn't go amiss.

18th | Bristol | Moment of Solidarity

Freedom News

Following a successful weekend for the Bristol Anarchist Bookfair and Radical History Festival more good news has come through from the south-west — solidarity donations to help homeless people whose tent city was burned down on September 9th have more than doubled the campaign target in less than a week.

The £1,000 cash drive by Bristol Homeless Action Movement, which aims to help replace the possessions of seven homeless people who had their tents burned while they were out eating at the Wild Goose soup kitchen, has raised over £2,600 at time of writing.

Bristol Housing Action Movement has a long history of working with Tent City; recently installing a solar panel and helping the residents set up an allotment. They said: "With winter a few months away it is very important that we provide the duty of care that Bristol City Council will not".

The arson, which took place in undergrowth around a mile to the east of the city centre, saw both tents and bedding set ablaze in what appears to be a very similar MO to several other burnings which have taken place over the last few months.

In June, a couple who had been living in a field next to the old Sorting Office in Cattle Market Road had their belongings burned when they went to get food, a week after a tent was torched in Castle Park. In July a homeless woman's possessions were burnt in front of her by Kingswood arsonists.

Bristol's homeless community has had a difficult time recently, as in addition to the burnings the local council has also been trying to oust people from parks. Last year Bristol council was heavily criticised by both campaigners and the sitting judge after they tried and failed to impose an injunction against tent sleepers in parks across the entire city — a measure mirrored by Brighton council this year.

Around 1,000 people are statutorily homeless in Bristol at any one time as of 2017, while a further 100 or so people were found to be sleeping rough during a research snapshot carried out in 2015 — up 1,200% compared to 2010.

OCTOBER

A test run of Universal Credit sees 80% of claimants fall behind in their rent payments, largely due to a "chaotic" administrative system. The government decides to press on with a general rollout.

9th | Manchester | Threats at the Adventure Playground

Freedom News

Andy Burnham's Labour administration found itself in yet another mess over homelessness today as it made its first abortive attempt to scare a self-organised homeless group off an occupied site in Hulme — just days after pledging to "end homelessness" in Manchester.

The spectacle has been particularly humiliating for City bosses because the squatted empty property was once better known as North Hulme Adventure Playground — a community space which was shut down by council funding cuts in 2014.

The council-owned land was occupied in August by around 40 people who had been evicted from Hotspur Press — itself an embarrassing episode for Mayor Burnham which prompted protests outside his office only weeks after his election on a ticket of helping rough sleepers.

Occupiers linked to Loose Space, who have nicknamed the spot the Addy, said in a statement today:

> "The county court bailiffs turned up to evict the residents, they spent over an hour watching and waiting, then called on Greater Manchester Police.
>
> "The number of people who came to support the attempt of eviction on the Addy meant that when they made contact this morning, with people up in the tree houses, the tunnels that were built and the solid line of activists, the bailiffs were made to change their plans as they were facing resistance.
>
> "The group made it clear that they would not be moved today, and that we were prepared to go to high court to seek a further ruling. This was another victory against the council, their eviction

policy and drive to gentrify Hulme. This would have not been made possible without the support from the Hulme community and the Manchester squat scene.

"Thanks to Lousy Badger Media for being there to livestream, Manchester Activist Network for their solidarity and our Liverpudlian family.

"Addy residents have spent the last two months at the site building small liveable spaces and planting seeds in an effort to make the space a community environment again, and have plans to transform the hitherto closed playground into a permaculture sanctuary. They've also stressed that they're well provided to resist an eviction, but would welcome people coming down to support".

9th | East London | On Predators

Andrew Fraser

There are many things worse and more dangerous and humiliating than being homeless. The third time I was made homeless, I didn't have much with me. Just a suitcase, a broken heart and my dignity. The latter didn't desert me this time.

I was down Stratford shopping centre, among the other waifs and strays. I had no sleeping bag but plenty of warm clothes. I couldn't sleep, apart from the blaring lights there were two guys lying near me, shaking, teeth chattering. I was more naive than I am now and I assumed they were cold. I got as many warm, clean things as I could find in my case and draped them over them. Turns out they weren't cold but on a drugs comedown. Still I'm glad I was able to bring them a little comfort. Yet it was another lesson waiting to be learned. Don't be visibly kind on the streets. Where everyone is fighting not to drown they will clasp hard to the strong ones and take you under the waves with them. Thus I met Alex. He'd been watching me and I was to be his prey. His meal ticket. He smelt my vulnerability and he pounced.

If you ask any homeless person they will all have met an Alex. For my friend Dmitru it was Sue. She worked for a charity. A lonely, needy soul, she pounced on him when he was at his most desperate. She worked for a charity that works for homeless people and she inveigled her way into his life and promised him a future which was dependent on him loving her forever. Her own love came with conditions. That, to me, is not love. It's just holding a vulnerable person captive.

He moved into her place and she got the ego-boost she required, but not the love. He couldn't possibly give that in such an unequal relationship. He had no freedom to feel, to be himself. There was only one set of keys and she held them. He knew very well that if he stepped out of line, he'd be back on the streets. Everybody steps out of line at some point and sure enough, the sheer pressure that comes from walking over eggshells with someone ensured that he did. And he was out on his ear. She somehow got my number because she knew I care about him. One day, after she had again locked him out in the cold, she called me blubbing and looking for sympathy.

"He used me" she sobbed.

"Yes and you used him" I told her. "Only difference is, you have a key. He doesn't".

That's the thing about us homeless types. If you take us in, you have to remember, we've gone feral. To survive. So it is not a promise you should make lightly. Our hearts are already broken so if you give us a place to stay then whip it away in a fit of pique, you will smash that broken heart to smithereens. And we might never recover. Mine is barely close to being healed.

One night I was sat with my mate Big Baz and his dog Reg in Ilford. Baz is the hardest man in Ilford, about eight foot tall, with about six teeth. A real gem. He's been homeless for 30 years. Imagine that. I met him when I still had a home and I was walking through Valentines Park, scratching my head because the government had stopped my benefits again for no reason. I was tired of the fight, when Reg, his beautiful Labradoodle came racing towards me and made everything alright. The way dogs do. Baz followed him.

"You okay?" was his introduction.

"No. You?"

Baz made me laugh until I ached. He didn't want anything from me but I managed to scrape together enough pennies to get us a few cans of beer and we laughed away our woes on the pavement near Tesco. He gave me something money can't buy, something that others couldn't give me. He gave me his respect and this man's respect was worth respecting. He told me I was his second best, best friend, after Reg and to this day that's probably the biggest compliment anyone ever gave me.

Anyway this one night I was sitting with him and Reg when this Yorkshire woman came by. She said she lived on a farm up north and she loved Reg and would Baz consider moving up there to live with her. His response was of course an almighty "yeah". He started to cry. He doesn't cry often, does Baz. I've seen him punch steel more times than I have seen him cry. But to anyone who tells you homeless people "don't want" a home, let me tell you, he leapt at the opportunity. And they do.

What he didn't see was the doubt in her eyes. But he was fair tipsy. I saw it. She suddenly realised what she was committing to and I knew she would never be back when she gave me £40 to share with him. 'This is my chance," he sobbed as she walked away. I gave him £20 but didn't dare tell him that she would never be back. Let him dream for a night. Which brings me back to Alex. Alex had a key to a door, a roof. And that's it. He had mortgaged every last thing he owned and he had somehow managed to swing himself a flat. It wasn't until later that I realised how.

His kindness was not kindness. He knew the exact day that I got my benefits and he would take more than half of them off me. Once, he claimed that he was going to buy a flat screen TV that never transpired (he hadn't even unpacked) another time, he claimed he needed money to pay his daughter's private education. Then every day, he would disappear with the solitary key (his power over me) and would emerge around 10pm demanding I bring him some cigarettes. So off his tits he could barely stand up and a study in projection, calling me a liar, a drunk, and a cunt. It's incredible how quickly you become acclimated to this kind of projection and abuse, simply because you've been rejected one too many times and you really don't want to believe someone else is doing it to you. And yes, you wanna keep that roof over your head. Like Dmitru with Sue, I WAS using him I guess. So much so that like Dmitru, I was prepared to put up with the horrible abuse of a sociopath.

I remember him being really "drunk" one night and telling me he was a very bad man. Seriously folks, if anyone ever says that to you, then run for the hills.

But Alex was greedy and it wasn't enough for him to be fleecing me. Soon he moved his nephew, George, in. George was also homeless and scared. Working night shifts after his marriage broke down and his cheating wife took the house. Alex didn't care, he was just another meal ticket. Instead of giving Alex money, I lied and told him the government hadn't paid me. Then I gave that money to George so he could have a good meal before he went to work.

We were all sleeping in that one room and I swear it was more horrible than any night I spent sleeping on the streets. On one Thursday morning I woke up and tried to run myself a bath. Alex awoke, went into the bathroom, removed the plug and called me, for the 149th time, a smelly cunt. And I began to cry. It's amazing how quickly a sociopath can break down your defences and your self esteem. Like a heat seeking missile.

I had already worked out his game at that point. He was on the gear. That's how he got housed. People on heroin get housed. I returned that night and stayed long enough to let his nephew in before Alex collapsed in a crack coma. I could have knocked him out with my little finger, but what would have been the point? George told me I had been more family to him than his own uncle and that made me feel proud.

As I left he finally managed to summon some humility.

"I'm sorry" he said.

"I don't care mate. You're gonna die lonely. Look after your nephew, he's more than you deserve".

There are many things worse than being homeless.

16th | East London | Heroin or Colchester

Andrew Fraser

There's a new shelter opening in Ilford next year thanks to the Sally Army. Real flats with their own toilet, kitchen, bedroom and living room. I won't ever be eligible for one, just as I'm not eligible for a council or housing association property. Just as I'm not eligible for any night shelters. There are myriad reasons but mostly it boils down to me being considered stronger than others so more able to cope with life on the streets. In some instances I agree, in other instances I see people being shoved to the front of the queue because they smoke crack and sit with their hands out. I try not to be bitter but it's horrible knowing that you are the bottom of everybody's priority list.

So I am left to the mercies of the Private Rental Market which no longer works for people like me on benefits because they are recovering from severe trauma. Most of that trauma was caused by homelessness which in turn was caused by the rampantly unregulated private housing market in the first place.

The biggest culprit, the biggest contributor to the soaring homelessness problem in the capital was the housing benefit cap. They used examples of people living in mansions with swimming pools and having their rent paid by the local council as an excuse to bring in the cap. The Tories' Liberal Democrat coalition partners were complicit in the cap and Labour town halls stayed strangely quiet, knowing the cap would save them a few bob. In terms of how it has destroyed lives this overlooked policy change was more wicked, even, than tuition fees.

Of course local government shouldn't have to pay for people to live in the lap of luxury. Those people should move somewhere more affordable. But the vast majority of people affected by this policy change were people living in modest homes who had lost their income due to ill health or misfortune. The cap is set WAY below market rates in the capital. I think they will pay up to £700 per month for a one bedroom flat in Leytonstone. The cheapest one bedroom flat is £1k a month and rising. Hence if you lose your job and you are living in private rented accommodation in London, you are effectively waiting to be made homeless because you will never be able to make up the shortfall.

And this is where I find myself now. Again. Facing homelessness. There is no available social housing. They were all bought by property speculators. And as I try to recover from my ordeal I am concerned that the room in the house with the toilet which I share with NINE other people costs more than they pay me in housing benefit. So, it's a matter of time before I get made homeless again through rent arrears. I am bottom of every priority list and you have to be living in the borough you've applied to for three years to even be considered for social housing. I haven't

(*Andrew lattery discovered that this information is untrue, despite being on the council website*). I've been homeless so I've moved around. I'm trying to get my life on track but it's hard when you don't sleep at night because you are so scared and scarred by the thought of being put back out on the streets again. The next time, if it happens, WILL be the last time because I've taken more than I can hold.

Meanwhile people leave London in their droves. The only thing that will save this city now is a rent cap. And a serious one at that. That will probably come too late for the likes of me and many others, talented teachers, nurses, artists and others who can no longer afford the insane costs of this city and are worn out from living an inch from the gutter while becoming increasingly aware that no one will help you if you do end up there.

Incidentally, why is it okay for private landlords to advertise their properties as "No DSS"? Would a shop or a hotel be allowed to do this? It's discrimination and you would not be allowed to make such stipulations about any other group in society. But then people on benefits know they are third class citizens with less human rights than others.

The problem has been labelled a housing bubble. But bubbles are nice and natural. It's a festering housing boil which needs to be lanced. Since the days of Margaret Thatcher, restrictions on the supply of homes as well as a completely deregulated private rental market which values landlords' rights above tenants, have led to property prices and rents going through the, ahem, roof. New house building plus rent caps would mean that house prices and rents fall to a realistic, human level ... some people will be sore. They had seen their flat double in "value" in five years and were under the misapprehension that they had won the lottery. But they were never really rich anyway, just property speculators who, knowingly or not, profited from an out-of-control form of capitalism which while enriching them was also destroying, both metaphorically and literally, the lives of others who didn't play the market quite so well. Or didn't even know what the market was. So, tough. What goes up, inevitably must come down. For the sake of the next generation as much as the homeless of today. For London, I hope the house price crash happens sooner rather than later.

And me, I guess I'll have to try to plough on here because to leave would risk having to go through the non-existent system all over again, with GPs, benefits, housing, housing benefits, social services. If I take a leap in the dark to save myself I could end up destitute again. But there's no doubt I'm in limbo.

I spent last week exploring the long term options and having spoken to all the many agencies allegedly there to help, it seems my only chance is to find somewhere in the private rental market. Finding a private landlord who takes DSS in London is like finding words of humility from Donald Trump. Even if I do find one, the chances of finding one who charges no more than the housing benefit cap, is somewhere between zero and infinitesimal. Which leaves me with heroin or Colchester.

Taking heroin would get me housed, most probably among people on heroin. But I'd be on heroin so I doubt I would be particularly arsed.

Alternatively, and perhaps somewhat more sensibly, there's Colchester. My friend at the Welcome Centre reckons she might be able to find me somewhere there. I've never been to Colchester but apparently it's quite nice if you ignore the casual racism and homophobia. But I'm sleeping in Dagenham, so I'm well used to that by now.

I'd be broken hearted to go. It helps with my depression knowing that I'm near old friends. The thought of tearing up my life and starting from scratch again is pretty terrifying.

But then again watching London, my onetime, one and only true love, die slowly in front of my eyes is often almost too sad to bear.

Gentrification, Brexit and the Housing Boil (tm) have conspired to destroy the things I once loved about this once-lovely beacon of European multiculturalism, liberalism, creativity and hope. A city which once inspired, enchanted and attracted people from all over the country and all over the world, now leaves the same people jaded and broken. If you're not winning in London, you're losing. It's a zero sum game.

Once, if you were tired of London you were tired of life. Now, it seems, if you value your life, you get out of London. Maybe it really is time for Colchester …

19th | Manchester | One-way ticket to nowhere

Freedom News

Following revelations that Manchester Council has spent £10,000 on one-way tickets to push rough sleepers out of the city, activists have been expressing their disdain for executives' excuses that the measure is aimed at "reconnecting" people with relatives who can help.

In a statement, Manchester Activist Network (MAN), which has been heavily involved in homeless self-organising in the city explained the real way in which the system works:

"Person becomes homeless. Person goes to local town hall. Person is told no housing available, all the money is in Manchester. Person goes to Manchester and asks for help. Person told they have no local connection, go back home. Person kicks off a bit. Person is offered a train ticket to stop them from staying in Manchester long enough to be considered as having a local connection (six months). Decision time. Go back to the place that's already failed you (and has a waiting list of two years) or stay and take a chance in a city where at least the public care even if the council doesn't.

"Either way there's no 'reconnecting' going on, if it were they would be following up each case and ensuring that the relevant services in the person's home town were ready for them. They don't. They pay for a ticket and that's the end of it.

"If there's one thing Manchester City Council does know how to do properly it's waste money, they're experts at it in fact. But whose money are they wasting? Yours. Ours. We must demand better".

The gulf between the promises of Manchester Mayor Andy Burnham and the policies of the city council have been growing ever more stark in recent weeks, following a spate of evictions of self-organised homeless groups, including of MAN activists, sometimes within days of new policies being announced that will supposedly "end rough sleeping by 2020".

20th | East London | The big issue with The Big Issue

Andrew Fraser

I hate the expression "virtue signalling". It's a very telling indictment of our times. That, somehow, to point out immorality or hypocrisy, makes you a prick because you're quite clearly trying to make yourself look good. Only a wrong 'un would think in that twisted way.

But as I sat down with my lovely Ukrainian friend Adrian, in the driving rain of Leyton tube station last night, I did feel that sometimes buying *The Big Issue*, and certainly managing *The Big Issue*, is a form of virtue signalling. I've done it myself and when I examine my conscience I do kind of understand where I was getting it SO wrong. You give 'em your £2 and you stroll off, confident that your conscience is clear. But it doesn't work that way, social responsibility to our fellow human beings is a debt that cannot be paid off with £2. It's about a bit more than just strolling past, chucking them a few quid, picking up your magazine and waltzing off to a dinner party.

Perhaps, we would be better off saving our spondooliks and actually taking time to speak to the person you believe you are helping. Last night Adrian asked me for money, I told him I'm a little short of it right now and I couldn't afford it. He looked at me with his big, soft, sad brown eyes which contain so many stories, and said: "Your friendship means more to me than any money you could give me". I felt bad, because I've been busy and haven't been thinking of him as much as I should have. But I also felt very honoured that he adorned me with the word "friend". That's priceless. I knew myself, during those cold, long lonely days that those people who just appear out of nowhere when you need to see them, the ones who sit down and chat to you … they re-humanise you, having been dehumanised by your experience. What those people give you in those moments is more precious than notes and coins.

The Big Issue depersonalises homelessness. It becomes just another commodity to be sold or bought. Armando Iannucci, the revered social satirist behind *Veep*, *The Death of Stalin* and *The Thick of It*, is the latest to grace its pages. He joins the well-meaning likes of George Michael, Woody Allen, Gary Barlow and many more.

The fact that these people give precious, valuable material to *The Big Issue*, when they could be flogging it to a glossy magazine, shows, on the whole, that their hearts are in the right place (unless it's a PR job to disguise tax evasion, for instance) but it also shows that they really are COMPLETELY out of touch with reality. Hadn't you noticed? Nobody sells *The Big Issue* anymore. At least not around East London.

The last time I saw someone flogging it was before I got made home-less again. My friend Craig in Romford with his little corgi Alice. He didn't want to sell it, but because "vagrancy" is still a crime and you can end up in the cells and have your dog stolen, for "begging" he had made the only choice he had. To sell *The Big Issue*. Sounds like a racket to me. The police had been harassing him and he was scared. But with *The Big Issue* in his hands, he was allowed to work his "patch". But only if he gave half his takings to *The Big Issue* which supplied him with the magazines which stopped him being arrested. Effectively, he and other homeless people are being taxed by *The Big Issue* and John Bird.

You could argue that, well, somebody has to pay the costs of produc-ing this increasingly threadbare magazine. Well, not really actually … *Metro*, *The Evening Standard*, *NME* and *Time Out* all survive perfectly well on advertising revenues. Why are homeless people not given this magazine for free? It's a gigantic scam.

Many years ago, I worked briefly for *The Big Issue* as a journalist. I didn't like it one jot. The holier-than-thou editors and chief executives were all on a nice little earner for their troubles and they got to look "nice" at dinner parties. They were pretty much all card-carrying mem-bers of the New Labour Establishment which ruled at the time. When it came to the end of year honours lists and peerages, they were quids in. They were handsomely rewarded. But for what? Did they eradicate home-lessness? Did they even try? Now that might mean killing the goose that laid the golden egg.

When I met Craig, he was in agony with his sciatica, no doubt ex-acerbated by the damp. "Seeing as you work for them, don't they send doctors to check you over?" I asked of *The Big Issue*. "They just drop the mags off, collect their money and piss off," he told me.

Maybe it really did start off with genuine intentions, but these days *The Big Issue*, like the Tory Party, is just an institution that exists to exist.

It's a big receptacle of people's collective guilt for not doing more. It does nothing to alleviate or solve the problem.

If you really want to help go and find Adrian or Craig or any of their mates and give them fifteen minutes of your times. You might even learn something precious. Maybe give them some cash if you can afford it and if you can't talk to them about ways you can help them access health services, maybe be an advocate for them as they wend their way through the horrendous benefits "system". If English isn't their first language, maybe be his or her voice.

And maybe, like last night with Adrian, just hold their hands for a while because they are scared. You will absolutely make his or her day, you might make a friend for life and you might even SAVE a life. And if that's virtue-signalling, I couldn't give a toss!

27th | East London | My friend Andreas

Andrew Fraser

He came to London from Eastern Europe, looking for a better life working as a taxi driver. But when his rent spiralled he ended up living on the streets. Then he started to take drugs to help him to sleep. Now he is desperate to give up and is looking for a path into rehab so he can begin his life again.

I am disguising his identity, because like many others, he is in a very vulnerable position. As a non-British homeless person he can be sent to one of the government's detention centres where he will be incarcerated and treated as a criminal and will have no recourse to legal help, *Panorama* recently screened a documentary about the ritual degradation and humiliation of vulnerable foreign nationals in these centres.

Andreas doesn't want to go back to his country because as bad as things are here, they are even worse there, where there is no money to help homeless people. "I would freeze to death on the streets," he told me.

He is a kind-hearted and gentle soul, he always offers me his food and sometimes even money and I see him handing out food to homeless people on a regular basis. He has a beautiful young daughter back home and he showed me pictures of his life before he moved to this country and everything went wrong. He looked happy and together.

Because of his precarious status, like other foreign homeless people, it is extremely hard for him to access services in this country and if he is attacked, robbed or abused, he cannot go to the police.

If anyone knows of an organisation which might be able to help him turn his life around, please let me know. He is deadly serious about giving up drugs. Whether it is here, or back in his home country, he doesn't deserve to die.

28th | London | An endless chattering

Freedom Journal

Recently the National Audit Office (NAO) published a study which was of surprise to no-one — notwithstanding the blustering pretend humbug of neoliberals and Tories — showing that welfare cuts cause homelessness to rise.

Not so long ago, this would have been a "well duh" report which would itself have risked being written off as wasteful government spending. But in reporting it for a 2017 audience the BBC duly pottered up to a government spokesperson for "fair comment," and were told by a presumably straight-faced PR weasel that they are "investing £550 million to address the issue".

This context-free and highly conditional "we're bunging money at it" line is, of course, one of the standard slate of PR responses that all governments try whenever the horrible consequences of their inhumanity get an airing on national television. Other tried and tested smokescreens involve telling us they're "disappointed" in the actions of the people making these reports, as though a naughty schoolchild has been caught writing something disgusting on the class whiteboard. Or talking about some vaguely noble-sounding piece of legislation which actually offers very little positive change — in this case, the "Homelessness Reduction Act," which nominally requires councils to help all eligible applicants rather than just those with a priority need but of course will be neutered by workarounds as councils have no extra real or ongoing resources to do so.

The numbers aren't really anything we don't know already. In seven years there has been a 60% rise in households living in temporary accommodation, including 120,540 children. That number is extraordinarily generous to the government, as it excludes everyone who is staying with family because they have nowhere else to go, have fallen through the cracks of the system, or simply don't qualify for "emergency" rooms even in extremity.

Around 4,000-4,500 rough sleepers were counted last autumn and noted in the same study — almost certainly a gross underestimate both then and now, given the notorious difficulty of doing comprehensive research on people who are by their very nature living beyond or actively avoiding the easy notice of bored researchers wandering around town centres. Nevertheless, that snapshot represented a 134% increase since 2010.

The NAO focused primarily on the impacts of cuts to benefits, which is of course a tempting way of finding correlation and causation, though it also said the main issue was the "ending of private sector tenancies," as rents have spiked upwards in London particularly amid the housing crisis.

Local councils, which have been decanting people out of major city centres for years now, have blamed a lack of support in building affordable homes. Charities concur, and add that benefit cuts exacerbate an already worsening situation.

All true. But all of these lines of attack miss the broad scope of what's happening in Britain — necessarily so, because the representatives of these great and good Opponents of Tory Austerity are of the same class and means as the people they castigate from their media pundit platforms.

Mixed motivations

When a representative of the Local Government Association responds to a question from a BBC journalist about the policies of a government department overseen by a Tory Minister, there is, most likely, no point at which an agenda isn't being satisfied for a middle to upper class figure making assumptions about people they don't understand.

The BBC reporter is looking for a quippy quote. Something snappy, which fits into the mold of the story. Council vs Commons. Charity vs Tory. Nice neat quotes from authoritative figures who know who they are talking to and what the requirements are in the studio. At some point, if we find someone nice and photogenic, we can do a case study about how miserable someone is — though the great unwashed aren't really suitable for the Daily Politics live, of course.

The LGA chappie meanwhile is pitching for his council chiefs against Westminster. His chatter will be all about the impact of cuts to the council allowance, a lack of power at local level, the impossibility of satisfying both Ministers' demands and constituents' needs. He won't of course, talk about systemic corruption and graft.

He won't talk about the dodgy development deals being stitched up by councils of all political hues, from Lambeth to Manchester, where luxury housing and gentrification are encouraged because they bring in far better rates for the coffers than affordable properties. Or about the measures taken to push rough sleepers out of sight and out of mind, park benches that can't be slept on, fines for begging, quiet words with the local cop shop to keep the smelly sods up at night. Shunt those homeless out to less powerful regions and we can drive the problem elsewhere, they don't say (but do).

The charity … well let us just see where their money comes from. Who it goes to. Follow the green paper road until we see the shine of those clutched pearls in the soft hands of their filthy rich executives. "The government must give more" these scions of wealth cry, as they pick up another bung to deal with the problem at rock-bottom prices in rotten brick hideaways, another contract to deal damage to the poor they "champion" via workfare or migration stitch-ups.

There are none so scathing of the Worthy Institutions as those who have to live with them, none so cynical of their intent than those who work on the shop floors for penny-pinched wages and are told "but this is a charity" when they complain, as though they have no right to live off their work while their chiefs rinse the piggy bank. Sixty per cent of donations on admin. Millions sat unspent. But please, "don't give money to beggars".

The "solutions" these people peddle are self-serving. They're patronising and cheap and short on horizons. They stumble around the nests of institutional power, endlessly screaming at each other about the foulness below because they can't for a moment admit that it's part and parcel of the edifice they have built.

Homelessness isn't just a result of poor policy in the management of State and capital, it's business as usual. Systemic. Capitalism is homelessness. For there to be a rich there must be a poor. If a very few own the land then everyone else must not. For one to profit another must spend, and thus, eventually, all but a handful are left wanting.

The rights and wrongs

When Westminster complains that it can't raise cash for housing or more resources for homelessness, it's half right. The logics of managing capitalism in Britain are limiting. Even a left Labour government can't solve the basic problem of higher taxation resulting in capital flight, the pressure of globalised production or the problems brought by massive borrowing — eventually it must bow to the needs of "responsible management".

When local government complains it's being stymied by Westminster it's thus also half right — pressure journeys downwards from the peak. But such councils are also expected to "manage responsibly" using their own bespoke taxation and their interests are therefore skewed towards those of the people who they get most of their resources from — businesses, homeowners. Certainly not from the homeless, regarded on the council balance sheet as little more than a drain and a nuisance.

When charities complain ... well they always complain. That's what they're there for, as long as they don't question core political and economic societal principles (they're legally bound not to). It's certainly not their role however to make themselves redundant, or to pass all the money to the poor. Heaven forfend that such feckless jobless louts be allowed to run their own affairs when trained, clever and stably employed people can do it for them.

An irony is that the Tories have ever said that State handouts reduce people's self-reliance, but a Rees-Mogg is always there to boast about the British impulse to charity, a form of aid requiring people to publicly define themselves as incapable of self-reliance.

The State-charity network as a whole acts simply as another cycle in the reproduction of capitalism. A 2011 study found that more than 15,000 charity bosses earn over £60,000 a year in this country, and 55 pick up more than £250,000 a year to "direct" the management of people whose lives they couldn't possibly understand. These are the thoroughly insulated decision-makers and gong-collectors for an 800,000-strong workforce trying to solve the insoluble while their bosses butter up fellow executives at glitzy events, saving the world one canapé at a time.

On collective self-reliance
Meanwhile the homeless themselves try as best they can to find their own solutions. They squat, they apply for limited hostel places or if unsure of Britain's complex laws and technicalities they sleep outside in tents and bags until the winter rolls around. They band together in little groups of mutual solidarity against the night, and hustle for the chance of a roof and a locked door.

We The People have never "owned" most of the land in this system, and progressively fewer of us own any of it, for it has been seized by those most aggressive hoarders of profit — wealth earned through ownership. And those space parasites leveraging their advantages to make yet more advantages cannot be done away with by capitalism, their greed is protected in its core and heart.

We do collectively have the power to take it back however — those 200,000 homes that have sat empty for more than six months, the luxury pads held over simply because the wealthy have nothing else to do with their cash than buy another concrete asset, the homes and flats that are gouged monthly for fat rent cheques. We The People have the numbers, the skills, and the productive power to not just tinker around the edges of a fundamentally unfair system but to remake it, throwing off the nets that are cobwebs for the rich and steel chains for the poor.

It has been done before with rent strikes and mass squatting campaigns. It is done today in occupations, eviction resistances and solidarity with the tent sleepers. In fights against the mismanagement of residential blocks and assertions of tenants' rights to control their own homes.

The war against capitalists' lust to dominate everything and everywhere cannot be won by letting the rich arbitrate our destiny based on endless studies they've commissioned which remind us all about symptoms we already see and refuse point blank to address root causes. It must, and eventually will, come from below — from the people whose lives depend on it and who have always been the true catalysts for lasting change.

NOVEMBER

Shelter reports one in 25 people are now classed as homeless in the worst-affected areas of England. The government says it's "determined to tackle all forms of homelessness" and Chancellor Philip Hammond announces the formation of a new Rough Sleeping and Homelessness Reduction Taskforce. Its remit will be to focus on halving rough sleeping by 2022 and eliminating it by 2027.

8th | East London | Some don't know how to give

Andrew Fraser

I was sitting at a freezing cold tube station with my friend Andreas the other night when this smartly-dressed black fella walked past and literally hurled some loose change at him. As Andreas scrambled to pick up the coins from the gutter, a younger black lad had seen what the first man had done.

"Oi, that's no way to give to homeless people!" he shouted after him.

Instead of being shamed, the first guy marched back, menacingly, towards Andreas.

"Well give us me fucking money back then," he demanded. Andreas sheepishly emptied the 62p he had collected in a paper cup back into the man's hands. The second bloke reached into his pocket, found a shiny new pound coin, and handed it to him. "I'll be back with more next time I see you," he told him. His kindness was the Alka Seltzer neutralising the acid aggression of the first passer-by.

I'd experienced it myself. A kind of angry form of giving which is actually an act of self-sabotage because it denies the giver that fleeting moment of satisfaction you get in knowing that you did something, not much, but something to make this shitty world a little less toxic.

When I used to sing up at Newbury Park station, I did get some who would fling a penny at me. I can't read their minds but I think it's fair to assume they were trying to disrespect me. But what they hadn't realised is that you can only disrespect yourself and if their intentions were cruel, then they surely succeeded. Anyways, I always picked them up. It meant I was a penny richer than I had been five minutes earlier. I would keep them in my back pocket as "lucky pennies". I still pick up pennies if I see them lying on the ground. It's my way of demonstrating to God that

I don't take for granted anything that I have and I never assume I will have money in my pocket. Because material security is just an illusion. I leave it to the universe to look after me and so far, it always has. I might have had a lesson or two to learn beforehand, mind.

It shouldn't be a surprise that we as a society are so fucked up about giving. At Christmas, look at all the effort that goes into making sure that you've bought a present for everybody who bought a present for you. That's not how to give. You don't give to get back. I know that the people who I give to, these days, will almost certainly never be in a position to give anything back and I wouldn't want them to anyway. I always say to them, if your fortune turns, then pass on this kindness to another. As others have done to me.

But this world is warped. There are those who give with malicious intent. My mate Big Baz was given a sandwich which turned out to have glass in it. Luckily, after thirty years on the streets, he's an old hand at the homelessness lark and he knew to check before he took a bite.

It was the sheer anger and hatred that certain people felt towards you for being broke which was really shocking. I'd love to know the psychology behind it. I suspect it's because those people feel they are losing in the rat race and fear you because you represent what they may yet become. And they resent us when we smile because although we have nothing and they apparently have everything, yet they're more miserable, anguished and resentful than we are. Gentle Andreas told me how a man had deliberately ground the heel of his boot into his foot the other day. It doesn't help that Andreas looks East European and it's been open season on people from that part of the world, from people of all communities, ever since Britain voted Brexit last year. White, black and asian Britons seem finally united in their disdain and often undisguised hatred of Romanians and others. Thank God Bonfire Night is out of the way, so Andreas will hopefully be able to sleep without having fireworks thrown on him. Still the celebration of the persecution and torture of millions of Catholics serves as a reminder that the UK is never more United than when it has a minority in its sights, be they homeless, East European, or both.

Which is why, more than anything, if you see us sitting in the streets, give your humanity to your fellow human beings, as well as a sandwich or a quid if you can afford it. Help them feel less alone, less exposed. Just by being there those few minutes chatting, you're setting an example to those with sheeplike minds to whom you are either invisible or the outright enemy. You might even afford them some protection in those moments.

And if you see someone getting harassed by the public or the police, don't get beaten up or arrested, but make your presence known. Shame them if you have to. Maybe take the side of life's ultimate underdogs, like the second guy did the other night. Give them a hug afterwards and if it's the police, politely ask them what they are up to (or do as I do and enquire how the fight against terrorism is going!). If they are acting aggressively, film them. Without the advantage of a locked door, which everybody else takes for granted, homeless people need the protection of the community which passes by. Just as that man showed in his short-lived and spontaneous reaction the other night. I don't know who he is, but I consider him a true hero.

14th | East London | Alex is gone.

Andrew Fraser

Previously I called him Andreas to protect his identity. But it's too late now. He's gone. So he's Alex.

He was taken by the police last week. Arrested for asking for help (vagrancy) and put on a flight back to Bucharest. No questions asked, no ifs nor buts, no legal help and no medical help as far as I know. Deposited back from whence he came and left to live or die. Theresa May wasn't kidding when she said she planned to make this country a "hostile environment" for immigrants. Still, effective genocide is a bit more than just hostile.

I got the news last Thursday as I searched for him to tell him the good news that I had almost certainly found him a place in rehab. Alex was desperate to give up the drugs and had begged me for help. He began taking them on the streets of London, after he lost his home because of a massive rent rise. But he was determined to turn things around, sort his life out for the sake, not least, of his young daughter.

London's streets had turned out not to be paved with gold. He had been spat on, stamped on and had a firework thrown at him.

"Why don't you go home?" I asked him one night. "It's horrible here".

"Because I will freeze to death on the streets of Bucharest," he told me. He wasn't exaggerating. Hundreds of people die in double figure sub-zero temperatures every Winter. I'd bought him a cheap mobile phone so I could keep in touch with him while I searched for somewhere to take him but from Wednesday I couldn't get through and I had a feeling something was very wrong.

The last time I saw him, probably the last time I will ever see him, I brought him two sandwiches and two pasties from the Sally Army which he gobbled down in about five minutes flat while we filled in his application for rehab online. Even in such rotten circumstances, he made me laugh. He was a gentle soul, always sharing his food with other people on the streets, often to his own detriment. One of the questions on the application form was "How have you survived so far?" and he replied, simply, "God".

We had a bit of a laugh that afternoon, despite the bitter cold, and I saw the light of hope in his eyes as we discussed his future. I said good-bye to him and he gave me a tight hug and said: "I love you. You are my best friend". I would struggle to find a higher compliment I've ever been paid, or certainly one that meant more.

He was five days from salvation and now he's in a living hell, IF he is still alive. God bless you Alex, I love you too brother. You will always be in my prayers.

DECEMBER

The Public Accounts Committee, a crossbench group of MPs, sharply criticises the government after new figures from the Department for Communities and Local Government noted yet another rise in the numbers of homeless households. The Department's snapshot found 9,000 people sleeping rough in England and suggested an overall rise in homelessness of 69% since 2010.

10th | East London | Performance

Andrew Fraser

I hate that word begging. It conjures up images of people prostrate on the pavement, on their knees, hands cupped before them. Please note, if you ever meet one of these people, usually dressed as old ladies or with a walking stick by their side, they aren't homeless. They're actually fit as a lop. I couldn't hold that position for five minutes (should I ever have wanted to). Street homeless people have more respect for themselves than that. I used to cheer myself up by standing next to them shouting "Liar! She's not homeless! He's not homeless!" They never dared challenge me. Stealing off people who need it more than them and giving the destitute a bad name. Can't be doing with those parasites.

"Begging" however, as I've said so many times before, is in fact asking for help. Which is a crime in this country. I have a friend locked up for just that right now. I "begged" a few times, but after that I used to sing and smile at people. That used to really throw some of 'em. You'd see them looking embarrassed, glancing furtively at you as they came down the stairs to the underpass at Newbury Park station where I would sit with my sleeping bag. "Sorry mate, I've got no change," they would mumble, like they had done something wrong. "I didn't ask for any mate, I was only smiling at you. You look like you need cheering up a bit". That used to really throw them.

I miss my days performing at that station, I really do. Every night, I stopped doing it when I had enough money to survive and enough to help people I knew who couldn't do what I did, so were counting on me for the fruits of my labour. Every day I would trudge up there, sometimes the bus driver would let me on for free when I showed them my sleeping bag, sometimes they wouldn't. No worries, a nicer one would usually be along shortly after. Buses and bus drivers are like people eh? You wait for ages for a nice one and then loads come along at once. I can't say I didn't dread doing it a bit, pre-performance nerves if you like. But I remembered some of the really shitty office jobs I've done and reminded myself that it was certainly less humiliating than that. And I drew strength from it. You'd always hope the first person who acknowledged your existence was kind. If they were horrible, it was hard to pull yourself around to carry on. There are people out there who want to humiliate or belittle you for being poor and you have to be resilient and not let them get to you. I knew that not many people could do what I was doing.

As a rule of thumb, 90% of people just ignore you — though I did make that hard for them by cracking jokes and offering them millionaire's shortbread (my little joke with myself). "It's role reversal night tonight," I'd chuckle and plenty found it really funny that a homeless man was handing out cakes. I loved it when they took one and walked on. At least they stopped. At least I was someone. Of the remaining 10%, I'd say 90% were nice and ten% horrible — which is certainly a better ratio than working in the media. I made friendships up there, people used to come to me for advice and healing. There was an old asian couple who ran a restaurant and used to haul great sacks of unused vegetables home every night. I'd spot them and run up the stairs and carry the bag down for them. They were a joy and they never gave me a penny, and I never expected them to. I didn't help them for that reason. I think they were skint too otherwise they'd surely have been in a taxi. But it was always lovely to see them. I hope they're okay and somebody has stepped in. After I stopped singing up there I felt really guilty that they would struggle.

And I remember loads of those nice people, the Romanian man who used to bring me delicacies from his home country, the young dandy who brought me a great big golfing umbrella so I could keep dry. I think I was singing, 'Why Does it Always Rain on Me') that night. The lovely asian lass who asked me about whether she should date this guy she'd just met and the woman who used to bring bagloads of food from Chop'd. It was a very spiritual place. Afterwards, if I'd had a good night I'd go off and share out my spoils. The give and take of existence. Just as life should be.

So rather than feel like a dirty "beggar" as some people undoubtedly thought I was, I was in fact, a cheeky beggar. I felt empowered like never before. Strong, brave and energised by learning to tune out the nasty people and breathe in those beautiful souls who didn't know me, but showed me the purest form of love. Perhaps I had found my forte in life.

After I got off the streets I was happy to see old friends, but some of them old "friends", if you catch my drift. They had seen me looking dirty and dishevelled. Well you would look like that too. And plenty ostracised me. Perhaps they were embarrassed for me, I dunno. I wasn't, I was proud that I had survived. It was usually the ones who talked a good game about kindness and socialism, yadda yadda, blah-de-blah. And yet other people, people who I perhaps wasn't as close to, really came good. Swings and roundabouts. There were a few in my life who clearly thought they'd heard and seen the last of me, and so treating me with blatant disdain was easy. Hey, sorry to disappoint.

And now they are forced to look at me looking (reasonably) respectable again. And they've stopped ostracising me. They treat me like they used to, with big hugs, a peck on the cheek and a piously inane enquiry as to my wellbeing. Not that those people will be reading this, but you know who you are. Deep down, I know you want to pigeonhole me as the loser who ended up homeless. But I take pride in my past. You have no idea how tough I am, tougher than you.

It seems mad to say, but I laughed a lot more during those days than I do now. Now, I have time to reflect on the fact that I was left for dead.

Back then, it wasn't about making it through another day, it was about making it through another hour. And I learned very quickly that sitting blubbing was not going to make my situation better. Smile and the world smiles back. When you're living your worst nightmare, there's nothing left to be afraid of.

There was this Catholic priest who used to walk past me up at the station. Just after the election, before she stitched up her grubby deal with the DUP, I used to sing songs about Theresa May. 'Ding Dong the Witch is Dead!' used to feature heavily and earned a few guffaws plus a few pound coins. He always used to look at me disapprovingly. He was a holy man and not one for such vulgarity I suspect. This one night I called out to him. "Father I've stopped cursing her," I told him. "In fact last night I prayed for her." He looked surprised. "That's good my son!" I couldn't resist. "Yes, I prayed she dies soon. Horrrrrrribly!"*

* Please note, before they send the rozzers around, I don't really hope she dies, horribly or otherwise, despite her and her government being responsible for the deaths of hundreds of homeless, poor and disabled. I do however, sincerely wish she'd fuck off though. And take the rest of them with her.

17th | London | No More Migrant Roundups

Corporate Watch

Migrants and campaigners scored a major legal victory against the government's anti-migrant Hostile Environment regime this week, as the High Court ruled against the mass roundup and deportation of East European rough sleepers.

In March, Corporate Watch published our report *The Round Up*, which revealed systematic collaboration between the Home Office, the Greater London Authority, local councils, and homelessness charities St Mungo's, Thames Reach and CGL to arrest, detain and deport Europeans nationals found sleeping rough in London.

Charity outreach workers, under contract from the councils, regularly carry out "joint shift" patrols with Immigration Compliance and Enforcement (ICE) officers to identify non-UK national rough sleepers. The report also showed how data collected by the charity workers and inputted into the London-wide "CHAIN" roughsleeper database was passed on to the Home Office.

The report further showed how managers from St Mungo's and Thames Reach were active partners in this collaboration from early on. It drew attention to documents in which St Mungo's clearly advocated working with ICE, applauding a "new approach in which immigration officials work with Local Authorities and outreach workers".

In the last nine months, North East London Migrant Action (NELMA) has spearheaded an active campaign against the roundup, supporting migrants under attack, whilst gathering further evidence and publicising the charities' collaboration. In November, working with the Public Interest Law Unit at Lambeth Law Centre, NELMA helped three men bring a judicial review of their treatment and the policy in the High Court.

On December 14th, Judge Lang found in their favour, ruling against the systematic and discriminatory profiling of rough sleepers. Crucially, she ruled against the Home Office's main justification for the policy: guidance issued since May 2016 which decided that someone is "abusing their treaty rights" as a European Economic Area (EEA) citizen if they are found sleeping on the street. The judgment specifically quashes this official guidance, sending the Home Office back to the policy drawing board. It may also open the way to substantial compensation claims from possibly thousands of people who have been detained and/or deported under that guidance.

Brexit targeting

This is a particularly important victory because the Home Office has used its "abuse" guidance to substantially increase raids against European migrants — a step coinciding with the move towards Brexit. The latest Home Office statistics show that 5,321 EU citizens were deported in the twelve months to September 2017. This is 47% higher than two years before; it is also a much bigger proportion of the total, as in fact deportations of non-EU nationals have been dropping. EU nationals made up 42% of the 12,560 people "forcibly removed" in the latest figures, as opposed to 26% (of 13,799) two years before. The same move is also clear in detention figures.

It's also there to see, more starkly, when we remember those who have died in detention. As the Institute of Race Relations reports, six people have died in Britain's immigration detention centres so far in 2017, the deadliest year yet recorded. Three were East Europeans. The names of two were Lukasz Debowski, died January 11th 2017, and Branko Zdravkovic, died April 9th 2017. Another as yet unnamed Polish man died in Harmondsworth in September. It is not yet known how these men came to be in detention. There is a high chance that they were picked up in rough sleeper raids, as these have become one of the Home Office's main weapons for targeting European migrants.

In short, it a real possibility that the court victory this week will save lives. The Home Office has said it will not appeal the ruling. But of course, it remains to be seen just how they will respond to the judgement. It could well be that right now Home Office lawyers are busy looking for ways to get around it and continue the roundup.

The scale of collaboration

Whatever the legal framework, the roundup relies on extensive collaboration from the charities doing rough sleeper outreach. Our report earlier this year detailed how this works on the ground through two main routes:

- Joint patrols, where charity workers and ICE teams go out together on the street
- Data sharing, where charity workers pass on data later used by ICE teams

Since the report came out, St Mungo's and other charities involved have tried to wriggle out from responsibility, making evasive statements to downplay their role. They have been helped in this by some inexact reporting. In August, The Guardian reported, based on information from Liberty, that ICE had access to a "map" of London rough sleeping compiled from data from CHAIN, the London rough sleeper database run by St Mungo's. This article claimed that charity outreach workers were "inadvertently helping the Home Office to remove people who were from the EU or central eastern Europe," as "the Home Office was given full access to the map for six months from September 2016, and that this was stopped only when homeless organisations found out and aired their concerns".

Such reports let St Mungo's and Thames Reach off the hook, even seeming to imply that they helped stop the roundup policy. The truth is quite different. To spell this out:

First, while frontline workers may indeed have been unaware of the role they were playing, charity managers have always known what was going on. This is amply proved by the documents cited in our March report. For example, minutes of the "Mayor's Rough Sleeping Group" show

St Mungo's and Thames Reach managers, amongst others, specifically discussing sharing CHAIN data with ICE in May 2015, as well as information sharing more generally.

Second, we are by no means convinced that data sharing stopped in March 2017. Whatever happened with that particular map scheme, the councils, charity contractors, and ICE continue to have regular meetings and share information.

Third, sharing CHAIN data was never the main issue. Joint shifts — where St Mungo's and Thames Reach workers go out together with ICE officers — have never stopped. Of course, in many cases they are written into the ongoing contracts between the local authorities and the charities. NELMA and others working in the field continue to collect testimonies of such joint operations.

New evidence on St Mungo's and Thames Reach collaboration
In fact, further documents continue to emerge revealing the depth of collaboration by St Mungo's and Thames Reach. Here we will mention two particularly striking examples. Both of these come from documents released under Freedom of Information requests, and recently sent to *Corporate Watch*.

One is St Mungo's bid for the current City of London homelessness outreach contract, which it was awarded in 2013 (St Mungo's outreach division was then called Broadway). The bid statement, written in 2012, shows that the charity was already enthusiastically working with immigration enforcement. The charity confirms that it "will work with enforcement agencies to tackle rough sleeping and anti-social behaviours," even promising that staff "don't see enforcement activity as a last resort or separate to [their] work, but as part of the process of supporting people off the streets". It specifically states:

"All Broadway Outreach Teams carry out joint shifts with police and enforcement agencies such as UKBA [now ICE]. For example, Broadway's City Outreach Team identifies geographical areas of greatest concern and then coordinates an approach with police to target resources in these areas".

There is a very similar approach in Thames Reach's bid for the Tower Hamlets contract, which it won in 2014 (the contract passed to St Mungo's in 2017). Thames Reach wrote that it:

"Has worked proactively with enforcement agencies across the capital for many years. Working closely with the UKBA [ICE] to achieve removals of A10 nationals [the countries that joined the EU in 2004] not fulfilling their treaty obligations is not palatable to some other teams. With Thames Reach, Tower Hamlets has a provider who has been working closely with the UKBA for some years, providing information for targeted operations and organising joint shifts".

These documents show both charities boasting about their collaboration with the Home Office long before this issue became public knowledge. St Mungo's say that all its outreach teams were doing joint shifts in 2012. Thames Reach in 2014 advertised how it was happy to do work others would find "unpalatable".

To repeat: while some frontline workers may well have been "inadvertent," or at least unwilling, participants, the charity bosses knew exactly what they were up to.

What next?

This week's court judgment is a real victory. It may well save some lives. But the campaign is not over.

The Home Office was already targeting migrant rough sleepers before it came up with the EEA "abuse of treaty rights" guidance in 2016 — as the two documents quoted above further evidence. The "abuse" guidance, now quashed by the court, allowed ICE to rapidly escalate that strategy, as part of a Brexit-themed shift to target more European migrants. But the Home Office arrested European rough sleepers before the abuse guidance, and it is unlikely to give up now. We imagine its lawyers and policy wonks are right now looking for new ways to justify the mass roundup.

Nothing suggests that St Mungo's and Thames Reach will end their involvement in the roundup. These two charities have been enthusiastically helping the Home Office with this for years. They evade or play this down in public statements — but gush about it in private documents looking to win contracts.

St Mungo's and Thames Reach get a free ride here if other charities and organisations turn a blind eye or make excuses for them. Last week, Crisis came out against the roundup policy. Many charity managers have criticised the roundup in private, but this was the first time a major homelessness charity had spoken up in public, breaking an uncomfortable silence in the sector. Organisations are of course linked by many partnerships, relationships and histories. But the hostile environment strategy is fundamentally about collaboration — making us all into part-time border cops. This means the very active collaboration of such as St Mungo's and Thames Reach — but also the silence and turning away of others.

24th | East London | Don't Ask For Help

Andrew Fraser

*Research from Buzzfeed just before Christmas found that 54 local
authorities had effectively banned begging in town centres, by imposing fines on people caught doing it. The councils involved were
split almost exactly down the middle between Labour and Tory, 26 to
27 with one independent. Birmingham, Newcastle, Sunderland and
Tower Hamlets in London were some of the safe Labour seats which
implemented bans.*

Never mind the number of prosecutions, it is the threat of arrest used
by "community bobbies" in collusion with local authorities, driving
homeless people from busy but relatively safe streets to "cleanse" the area,
which causes the most damage. Also thousands upon thousands are arrested, have dogs taken off them, then released without charge because,
well, the police can. It's in the law. It's a form of harassment. But it goes
entirely undocumented. Aren't there terrorists to catch?

Corbyn, we expect this of Tory authorities, but if you really aspire
to make Labour a party for the many, not the few, then get a grip on
your local authorities which are more often than not, the worst offenders.
And put the repeal of the Victorian vagrancy laws at the heart of your
manifesto. Otherwise you and your party are just playing to the gallery.
All of my worst experiences in urban London were under the auspices
of Labour Town Halls. "Not being as bad as the Tories" doesn't wash
anymore and it's not even true when it comes to local government.

• • •

Here We Are Again

You might notice that homelessness is all over the media right now. It's an annual thing, part of the festive pantomime where society pretends to care. Like Christmas lights, we're picked up in mid-December, then thrown back in our boxes long before twelfth night. I'm not a fan of the term "virtue signalling" but when it comes to politicians and rough sleepers, I think the cap fits.

Anyway just to keep you all up to speed, the Mayor of London has just announced an initiative to build a project to aim for a programme of initiatives and projects aimed at eventually taking some people who sleep outside and putting them somewhere inside. Or something.

Presumably he'll call upon some of the UK's most brilliant minds, who will sit around drinking coffee and pondering how on earth we can possibly find safe and dignified shelter for tens of thousands of rough sleepers in a city overflowing with empty and disused properties. It's a truly Herculean proposition. Perhaps he should call in Stephen Hawking, but then if his answer is the same as mine — errrm, put 'em indoors, then it might hardly be worth the fee.

The Mayor will be talking to 18 homeless charities about what to do next. London has many, many public buildings which could be opened up all year round so that nobody has to sleep outside. It beats me why it takes 18 charities, all the combined resources of the many London boroughs and national councils, the national government and the Mayor of London to solve this problem. If I'm being simplistic then it's entirely intentional. The short term solutions that we require need to be really simple.

Mind you, all these organisations employ thousands of executives on big fat salaries. Is it really in their interests to fix this once and for all? Many would be out of a job. The proverbial turkeys who voted for

Christmas. I bet if they were told they would be sacked if they didn't do something, then solutions would magically appear. Requisitioning of empty public and private properties should happen immediately as befits a national emergency. Four people in Ilford alone have already frozen to death this winter. Where is the public enquiry? Local authorities, government and police should be investigated and if necessary face criminal prosecution, as with Grenfell and Hillsborough, if they have failed in their duty and allowed precious lives to be lost needlessly.

Meanwhile, back in the real world, Christmas is actually one of the least bad times to be on the streets, providing it's not too cold. Imbibed with Christmas spirit, the people who normally walk past you suddenly notice your existence. I'm not sneering. It feels nice, but you are well aware you will become invisible again long before the tinsel comes down and the sense of shared humanity will melt like snow on Boxing Day.

There's a lovely lady sits up Gants Hill who I saw being accosted by a well-meaning but exceedingly drunk woman at the station two nights ago. "Good on ya girl," she staggered and slurred. "I don't care WHAT you're on, you're shhhtill human".

I glanced at the homeless woman and winked and she laughed and shook her head. We could both guess what the drunk lass was on, about nine Bailey's and five blue WKDs I'd wager. Still, at least she took the time.

So what should you give a homeless person for Christmas? Give them what you'd want if you were out there. So if you're planning on stuffing your face this Christmas, take them some roast potatoes and leftovers. If you smoke, give 'em a few fags.

And if you like a drink, buy them a beer. If it's good enough for you, why not for them? I saw a couple of homeless blokes in the same spot last night having a beer and a cigarette and laughing and joking. It really wasn't what the passing melee wanted to see. And few hid their disapproval, even though they were probably on the way back from the pub themselves. We're allowed to smile too y'know. It's actually the best, the only way to stay alive in that horrible situation.

And if you really want to help, maybe think about befriending a homeless person in the New Year. Sit down with him or her, find out how they got there, and see if maybe you can give them a lift climbing up that greasy pole which might one day take them off the streets. Escaping homelessness is a labyrinthine task, but two heads are better than one.

And maybe forgo that gingerbread latte, or the entirely unnecessary festive doilies you were planning to buy and give the money to someone who might appreciate it more than you. You'll feel a rosy glow far better than you'd get from the latte.

And it being Christmas, why not spend a bit of time pondering what the world's most famous homeless family, Jesus, Mary and Joseph must make of how we treat our poorest and most vulnerable as we sit down and stuff our faces.

There are many things about Christmas which really are abhorrent, too many to list here. But it is known as a time of giving. The truest form of giving, I believe, is to those who we don't know. Those who we know will never be able to pay us back.

Wishing you a happy Christmas and thanks to all of you who have shared and supported this blog during 2017. Hey, I'm still alive!

31st | East London | New Year's Resolve

Andrew Fraser

So what's your New Year's Resolution? To travel more? Lose weight? Find the relationship of your dreams? Stop smoking? Quit drinking for a bit?

After the traditional orgy of consumption that is New Year, following the Christmas gluttony of a week prior, it's traditional to hand-wringingly pretend to give something up — for a few weeks at least.

But if you're a rough sleeper or precariously poised just above the water-line, paddling hard to avoid slipping under and feeling like someone has chained you to a sack of potatoes, you don't bother with such fripperies. New Year is not about what you give up. It's about not giving up.

I thought about this, this week, as I worried about my friend Alex. Kicked down too many times to mention, a childhood nobody deserves and a lifetime spent trying to overcome the aftermath of that, and all the insults to injury which follow, delivered by those who know even less than they care.

Having given up the heroin and then methadone, but without a penny to his name, he was arrested and incarcerated for begging. Slung into a prison where crack and Spice is as freely available as candy in Disneyland. I have no way of contacting him now. I wanted to speak to him, to try and let him know he's not alone and to continue his lonely fight to recover from a trauma which was not of his making. But I'm not allowed. I cried for him but then realised how useless that was. He either will or won't succumb. How can someone keep going when they've been repeatedly been kicked in the teeth? Then I remembered. I did.

It's true. What doesn't kill you makes you stronger. But sometimes it's a close call. When you're under attack by evil fuckers who don't care if you live or die, and would most probably prefer the latter, something awakes inside you. Not just the survival instinct. Anger. And channelled right, my God you can knock those aforementioned fuckers off their feet.

These days I can breathe a bit easier, but back then, sleeping behind the bins, or wherever, the day began, bleary-eyed about 7am, an hour to come to, go and see if I could find some half-smoked cigarette dimps, then fight. Dragging my arse from GPs to housing to benefits, throw in a social worker maybe, up to the station to sing, maybe do some writing if I had time, go to the Sikh temple for food. Keep smiling, keep laughing, keep going. Don't let the bastards win. Bob into McDonald's to use the toilet and weep silently in the cubicle, then onwards and upwards.

The task of getting back on my feet seemed impossible. I knew that the government and council never would help me but I also knew that the minute I gave up, I'd be dead. I never worked so hard in my life. I even considered trying to get sectioned so I'd have somewhere to sleep and they might have to house me afterwards. But I'd seen people coming out of mental wards lobotomised by whatever they'd put them on to shut them up. That wasn't for me. I'd sooner die than live some kind of half life with the pharmaceutical industry controlling my brain. I was never mad, but I was very disturbed by what had been done to me. Still am probably but it's wise to know thine enemy. Sadly there are people who are willing to grind their heels into your fingertips as you cling on for dear life.

And then I got lucky. Except I don't believe in luck. I prayed a lot because I knew very well that I needed a miracle to sweep me from harm. It was no use relying on Theresa May. She hates my kind. Time for someone a lot more powerful.

And I believe he sent me angels in human form. I lost count of the number of times I bumped into the exact right person just in the nick of time. I spend a lot of time here railing against governments and councils but even they are staffed by individuals, some good, some bad. I'd say a prayer before every appointment, that this one or that one wouldn't be an actual sadist — and I actually began to realise that when these individuals tell you they "can't" help … they actually mean they won't. They can, and if you are lucky enough to draw one of the benign ones out of the hat, on that fateful day, one single person can save your life.

Sitting on my sleeping bag up at Newbury Park station, the kindness of strangers absolutely saved my life, my sanity and my belief in human nature. Our actions are extremely powerful when directed towards someone in need. We can all do that and we may never know just how a hand on someone's shoulder or a kind word, can save someone from something terrible. Follow your instincts.

And among the many songs I used to sing at the station, this was the one which helped me the most. I used to look at people stumbling off the tube and through the tunnel and see the trauma in their eyes and I knew there were many, sleeping in actual houses, under actual roofs, with real front doors, some earning huge amounts of money, who had it much worse than me. I was smiling and laughing at least. And in my darkest hours when I listened to this song, it felt like I was listening to angels.

To all of the people here reading, who have kindly followed and supported this blog, that's my celestially-sent New Year's advice to you, whatever you're facing.

Life is never easy, nothing worth having ever is. If you're stuck in darkness the best way to banish it is to laugh, sing and dance. Really it works.

Keep your head high and your heart strong, let go of the past and stay in the light.

And never mind all those twonks telling you what you must give up. Do it in your own time. Just keep dreaming, keep believing in magic and don't, ever, ever, give up.

JANUARY

Spikes and bench furniture designed to deter homeless people from sleeping on them draw national condemnation, particularly after rapper Professor Green films a video of activists removing an anti-homeless bar from a bench in Bournemouth. "Again, nothing done to tackle the problem, just something to make it more invisible so we can pretend it isn't happening," he says.

1st | Bournemouth | The Exeter Road Occupation

Freedom News

Organisers in Bournemouth who took over land earmarked for luxury housing and turned it into a sanctuary for the homeless over Christmas are preparing to defend themselves against an eviction attempt tomorrow.

The ground on Exeter Road, opposite the Bournemouth International Centre (BIC), is likely to be subjected to a dawn raid by bailiffs and activists with Occupy Bournemouth are asking supporters to turn out from 6am — though people are also welcome to camp out. Talking to *Freedom*, a member of the occupation group explained:

"We are being crippled by the corporate greedy council, John Beesley (council leader) and his gang, carry on passing planning permission for luxury apartments and holiday homes, with his own company Quantum Group getting big residential home contracts, whilst ignoring the rapidly growing homeless problem we have here in Bournemouth.

"Occupy Bournemouth wants to take a stand and on December 13th we did that, occupying a largish bit of land where a Methodist church used to stand in the town centre, ironically enough due to be turned into luxury flats and holiday homes.

"We made it into a sanctuary for the homeless, where they'd have a safe place to stay and have warmth, food and shelter. It was timed in a way where we'd know they'd have a safe place for Christmas.

We now have around 30 homeless people on site, who would have been sleeping on park benches and shop doorways in the freezing cold, who now have a safe place to go with onsite first aid equipment, food and water in abundance and the kind donations and offers of kindness keep on coming!"

"The response from the community has been just amazing, people coming from all over neighbouring Poole and Bournemouth to drop down donations and give their time cooking, cleaning and welcoming residents and guests. It's a wicked vibe in camp and so amazing to see.

"It's a totally peaceful protest and stand that is really important to us, this is about raising awareness to the community and showing our corrupt corporate council that we will not tolerate the misspending of our taxes anymore.

"The Sanctuary has an eviction notice set for January 2nd any extra bodies which may be needed to take a stand would never be turned down".

The site, which is currently hosting around 30 people, has been cleared to foundation level so is basically a big pit, but it's nicely enclosed and reasonably safe. Because of community generosity the site is relatively well provisioned and is only infrequently making callouts for sundries, mostly things like coffee, fuel and milk, though a generator would be useful for power. There are also plans to begin longer-term fundraising to get rough sleepers in the camp indoors as the weather turns colder.

2nd | Bournemouth | Gone

Freedom News

The eviction went ahead this morning. Several videos were taken of the bailiffs coming in and destroying the site facilities. An owner turned up along with the eviction crew, and spent some time explaining to the people he was evicting, one of whom had just given him a cup of tea, that "there's nothing I can do" and "I'm just like you".

FEBRUARY

The BBC reports that homeless people who qualify as homeless and in need of housing support are being "unlawfully turned away by councils, despite their statutory duty". Support charity The Legal Services Agency reported that they saw about 200 people turned away in Glasgow alone in 2017.

A rough sleeper dies in Westminster Station.

The government's "anti-homelessness task force" is yet to hold a meeting.

5th | East London | Rosie and Callum

Andrew Fraser

Rosie

She's a lovely girl, Rosie. Fallible, y'know. Like us all. But a good soul and a kind heart.

She's got four kids. Single mum. People judge people like Rosie but I see how hard she works. Keeping it all together. Sometimes she messes up. She's tired you see. And don't we all need to be free enough to make bad decisions once in a while? And she only does it once in a while. And she's still young. And if you can't make mistakes when you are young, then when can you?

I suppose, if I was the *Daily Mail* I'd ask, "Why did you have all those kids when you couldn't afford them?" And the answer is, she's a great mum, with a lot of love in her heart. She just happened to attach herself to the wrong bloke who ran off and left her in mountains of debt. Then she couldn't afford the rent, then she was slung out of her home. Then she was put into temporary accommodation. Those places are bestial and certainly no place to raise children. One of her daughters has already tried to commit suicide because of what they went through there.

Anyway, after a couple of years she got out of there and into private rented accommodation. She got behind with the rent this year. Not because she's feckless. Because it's hard. They took her to court but she had already found a second job (she already works 30 hours a week and tries to bring up a family). She told the court she could afford to pay an extra £50 a week. Might not sound much to you but it's about seven extra hours a week to her. Hours she didn't have. Her mum's just had a stroke. But she would have found 'em. She's resourceful. And strong. And brave.

Anyway Dagenham Housing fought her. When it went to court she had no legal representation. She couldn't afford it and she thought they would let hear off on humanitarian grounds. You live and learn.

She's got to be out of the property in two weeks. They will return her to the the bedlam of a hostel. If they are lucky they will get the privilege of a couple of rooms. She already had a home, which she made nice. She even sorted out the black damp which the landlord refused to do, out of her own pocket. Well she couldn't have her kids getting ill. Now they're gonna move her out and somebody else in? Why?

You do the maths. It makes no financial sense to do this. Morality should rule but sadly it doesn't. But it doesn't even make financial sense. Her kids are going to become poorly. Some of them may turn to crime or drugs. She may have a breakdown. Then the kids will have to go into care. This will all cost money. Rosie thinks she's being punished. I think so too. But what for? Why do these faceless people hate her and her children so much? You tell me.

Callum

Just before Christmas our esteemed Prime Minister Theresa May made an important distinction in the House of Commons. There are two kinds of homeless, she pointed out. So when they say there are so many hundreds of thousands of homeless people in this country, they don't mean people without actual roofs over their heads. Some of them do, indeed, sleep under a roof with a door.

She felt it necessary to point out that fact and the fact that there are no children sleeping out in the cold. She was correct. You have to be a 17-year-old boy or girl before our society will grant you the privilege to freeze to death on the streets of our cities and towns. Rule Britannia. Theresa, I'm so proud of our nation.

Around the same time as she made the speech, I met Callum, 22. I told him I'd been homeless and he told me he'd been homeless too. But then when I said I used to sleep in graveyards and such, under the wall behind the police station, behind Marks and Spencer, he apologised. He was making the same distinction that Theresa May was making. He'd never actually slept out in the cold.

Nope, Callum was one of the "lucky" ones. He spent his entire teenage years growing up in temporary accommodation you see. Where Rosie and her kids are being packed off to, in two weeks.

Lovely lad Callum. A gentleman. He could have been something great. He's still fighting to be that man but he's weighed down by the sins of the past. Not his sins, I hasten to add. He used to be a drug dealer but his innate decency somehow broke through the chains of poverty and that sense of just fighting to survive, for his mother and sisters too. He was the man of the house you see. Except there was no house. Just two rooms which they all grew up in together. And there was no money. And dealing drugs was easy money, so that's what he did. Why wouldn't he? All the other lads in all the other rooms around him were, so why not him? He could make enough to buy presents for his mum and little sisters and he wasn't actually using the drugs, so why not. Then when he was 20 somebody died from the drugs he had sold and he fell apart.

Now he's training to be a carpenter. A real job. He has a beautiful girlfriend but he whispers to me that he finds it hard to maintain relationships because of the guilt he feels and the fact that he grew up in an environment where, at 14 years old, there were older prostitutes offering themselves to him so they could get the money to buy drugs. He never said yes but that was not a good introduction to the sexual world for a young man and he admits he struggles with not objectifying women. His girlfriend arrives an hour after we meet and he pleads me with not to tell her any of this. Of course I won't. He can't tell her because he is filled with shame and he just wants to look forward. Fair enough. He's a broken angel Callum, I reckon.

10th | East London | Spinning Around

Andrew Fraser

Driving through the driving rain on a stinky skunk-scented bus strewn with chicken shop debris I remember that night, sleeping down Stratford interchange. And I smile. Broadly.

You see I had lost everything. And I mean everything. All I had was my sleeping bag and £50 in the bank, which was more than most people had down there. I should have been despondent, terrified, broken … but I really wasn't. Perhaps it was the reaction to potentially having lost my life three times in four days. Perhaps I just didn't care any more. But it felt like ecstasy.

There was music playing, and skaters whizzing around and around the centre and it felt like a carnival of the destitute. I cracked open a beer and I started to laugh and dance and sing. This was ridiculous huh? I don't know if it was the skaters whizzing past but I felt like I was on wheels myself and then I felt like I was flying around the dowdy shopping centre like a happy dove, a beer can and a cigarette dangling from my beak. And the shopping centre suddenly didn't look it's dowdy self. It felt like the best nightclub I had ever been in. And then a thought hit me, this feeling of pure bliss that I'd never before felt. Perhaps I had in fact died over those last four days. Perhaps this was heaven. Yes, that was it, I must be in heaven. And us lot at the bottom of the pile had indeed inherited the earth. In which case just go for it. I did.

And in that half forgotten moment I think I temporarily transcended this world. Transcended all the fear that was bred into me. I was alone with my soul and God and the music, as the cheap shops flew by. And it changed me forever, somewhere deep in my bones, something most other people will never understand. Because they've never been so luckless.

And I was fine. I have never been happier. Free of all the judgement. Free of judging others. The chains had melted like butter.

So when you see me rush in where angels fear to tread, saying stuff that you're really not meant to say, refusing to abide by the rules, my own worst enemy eh? And you tsk and roll your eyes and say, stubborn bastard. Well ha! You don't actually know me now. As long as I know I have done my best, been kind, showed love, then I fundamentally don't care. Really deep down I don't. I know, that is where I am at my most free. That is the place where I lose my ego and just return to that perfect moment somewhere in suspended animation. Deep, deep, deep, deep down, I'm not scared and I'm not actually here. Just spinning through the universe somewhere. My spirit can fly away from this place and go somewhere better and leave the mortal me behind at any point. And he, of course, will be judged afterwards. And let them. But really. REALLY. Who cares?

I know how to fly.

UK NEWS & SQUATTING ROUNDUP

OOP NORTH – Manchester's squatting resurgence continues unabated, exploding from the Cornerhouse's monthslong festival of occupied art and culture last year into a budding community of buildings organised for purposes of HEALING, ACTIVISM, ARTS and KETAMINE. Highlights include taking the WONDER (HOW THEY GOT) INN once it closed as a venue and the rugged majesty of the HULME HIPPODROME. Pop up for a cuppa once London gets too gentry.

LAAANDAAAN - people haven't been too slack what with the Sofia Solidarity Centre in W1 being opened up through the onslaught of the Beast from the East and providing food, clothes and shelter to over 60 people each night. And in Montague Square, a bunch of plucky students have occupied part of the British Museum and are running Radical Residency programmes for the week running up to court. CHEEKY

DAHN SARF - WINTER CAN BE A PIG'S ARSEHOLE in squatland at the best of time, but let's give a mad shout of support to the BOURNEMOUTH SANCTUARY where a group of more than two dozen self-organised homeless peoples been keeping the spirit of OCCUPY alive by taking disused land and filling it with tents and makeshift facilities much to the disgust and panic of the Powers That Be. Despite a violent eviction at the beginning of the new year, they continue to hold a space for supporting people sleeping rough and trying to get into temporary accommodation.

Let's have a games night, New social space open around Charlton Area, looking for people for Circus Group and theatre. Also if anyone else wants do workshops or events, that they a need space for you can contact them Contact: 07397841654.

Copies of the SQUATTER'S HANDBOOK are also going to different places across the country, distributed by interested folks who see that squatting can be a direct solution to homelessness. Distributing stuff for free? That sounds like something SLAP could do with help from HINT HINT YA LAZY SCRUBS ...

MORE OOP NORTH - Speaking of the 'Drome, over in LIVERPOOL the scrappy scousers are still holding on to another building formally owned by the sleazy christo-maggots of Gilbert Deya Ministries. From all reports, the North seems like a squatting gold-mine, with vast numbers of empty derelict properties just waiting for the right kinda scamps to put them into good use and take direct action against the current housing catastrophe. NICE ONE ARE KID

Got news on squatting in your area? Drop us a line and an update to squatterslap@riseup.net ... send us stuff in and get entered for our raffle to win AN ACTUAL CROWBAR!

MARCH

The "Beast from the East" cold snap prompts a record number of homeless alerts across Britain. The following month, a tally of the death toll by the Bureau of Investigative Journalism finds 78 people died over the course of the winter.

14th | Bournemouth | Chased

Freedom News

The Sanctuary occupied homeless camp on Ashley Road, east Bournemouth, was evicted yesterday, leaving rough sleepers struggling to find anywhere safe to stay or put their belongings. The camp was the second set up by homeless people working with Occupy Bournemouth activists in the wake of a New Year eviction of a site on Exeter Road, opposite the Bournemouth International Centre (BIC) in which bailiffs tore down and crushed people's belongings despite freezing conditions. An Occupy activist said:

> "Bournemouth council's attitude towards homelessness is disgusting and … with the change in legislation coming up we have a chance to support/advocate for, all our homeless to get housed".

The site had been under threat since last month, when owners Brightmark Ltd were granted an eviction notice — it's tipped to become a car park.

The new Sanctuary closure is just the latest in a series of setbacks for rough sleepers in the area, who lost direct access to the local night shelter three years ago and have since had to rely on groups such as St Mungos, which have been hit by a scandal over information sharing with the Home Office. Many homeless people have lost trust in such organisations as a partial result — an issue not helped by what campers say have been repeated attacks by St Mungos on Sanctuary over the last few months.

Only last month, Bournemouth council was forced to backtrack on its installation of metal bars on benches to stop homeless people from sleeping on them, which became a national embarrassment after rapper

Professor Green took direct action to remove them and 17,000 people signed a petition against the policy.

16th | East London | Life of Surprises

Andrew Fraser

Never let your conscience be harmful to your health
Let no neurotic impulse turn inward on itself
Just say that you were happy, as happy would allow
And tell yourself that that will have to do for now …

I woke up angry that day. I am not angry now. Anger lets them win. Lets THEM in.

I was sleeping at the McCreadie Hotel, Forest Gate. Shithole. But a shit hole with a roof and a door which locked. More than I had had three days earlier. Sleeping outside M&S in Ilford, with them playing a pigeon alarm to disturb us all night because clearly we were vermin.

After two and a half days of physical collapse, pissing in the sink because I could barely stand let alone stagger to the toilet down the corridor, I woke up. All I could hear was the sound, which I had been hearing subconsciously for two-and-a-half days of the crackheads in the room next door screaming at each other. I looked down for my mobile phone, so I could call the people I love to let them know I wasn't dead. And the mice which I had heard scrabbling around my bedroom floor had eaten through my charger.

Anyways, I woke up no longer tired but still hurting and my body weak because while I had been sleeping for two and a half days because of shitty Marks and Spencer I haven't eaten during those two and a half days and my brain isn't working.

And I scream. And I cry. And I shake my fist at God. He had saved my life on so many occasions. But because I was so poorly my mind could not remember them. The time I had to get up out of my sleeping bag at 6am to go sing at Newbury Park station, when I really weren't in the mood and it was a forty minute walk away and I had no money for the bus and needed nicotine because I was addicted to it and stressed.

And on the way, as I looked for dimps to smoke I found an unregistered Oyster card which had £13 on it. Yay! Happy days!!

Or the time I had my sleeping bag and my piece of material which I called a bed in a cheap bag from Lidl and had made enough money that day from singing to buy myself a pint. This bloke looks at my scruffy bag and scoffs "Who left the washing out". And I look him straight in the eye and say "that aint no washing that's my bed you cheeky fucker." Anyway, turns out he was a lovely bloke named Paddy from Nottingham who bought me a couple of drinks and let me sleep on his floor that night.

Or the night I met my beloved brother Saul who saved my life twice when he barely knew me. We had only met once, in suspicious circumstances, but the first time I saw him I knew he was special and I guess he must have seen that in me because he took me in for a night, let me have the dignity of a shower and festooned me with clean clothes. All these things and about a thousand more I have not yet mentioned were miracles not coincidences. So I knew very well that God exists. But at that moment all I could hear was the crack addicts screaming next door and all I could think of were all the broken relationships I had had which had been destroyed by stupid money. And I screamed. "Why? Do you hate me?? Why the fuck did you let this happen to ME???"

And he said

Because you asked for it

"What the fuck," I shouted

"I asked for THIS? You mean I deserve it??"

And he said no. But you did ask for inspiration and I gave you a gift as a writer not just to make money or write silly jokes. Because that gift is also a responsibility. To tell the truth and shame the devil. I hope to my soul that I'm getting somewhere with that.

22nd | East London | We won!

Andrew Fraser

On March 17th the Ilford branch of Marks & Spencer announced a local initiative to help rough sleepers. The efforts a year before of homeless people, including Andrew Fraser, to stop the shop using an alarm to deny them sleep and drive them away had forced its man-ager to admit it was wrong. Amid a wave of bad press, the firm even-tually made amends by collaborating with the council to provide "a pop-up hostel in the form of 42 studio flats in shipping containers on land provided by Redbridge council". According to M&S's PR bumf, this was the first time in its 130-year history that the retail giant had made any such attempt to help the homeless.

Those of you who have been following from the very beginning will know that THIS is where it began. I was one of those rough sleepers tortured by that alarm and through this blog, and your support, we got it stopped. Sometimes it feels like I am screaming into a wind tunnel. But WE did this. God bless you all for your support and PLEASE keep sharing and I will keep telling the truth.

AFTERWORD

ROOTS OF THE ROOFLESS

Andrew Fraser's diary lays bare the stark reality of homelessness in Britain in 2018. Things that the rest of us take for granted, a roof over our heads, access to electricity to charge a phone, the ability to cook a simple meal, clean pillows, become luxuries for Andrew. And of course he is far from alone — rough sleeping has risen by 169% since 2010[1]. There is also a large increase in the number of women sleeping rough; they now officially account for 14% of the total. Andrew explains clearly the additional risks faced by women on the streets.

At the same time many of us are not far away from ending up on the streets with nowhere to live. According to Shelter, 8.6 million people could not pay their rent or mortgage from their savings for more than a month. Over half said that if they lost their job, they couldn't pay their rent or mortgage at all. The research reveals that families with children are in the most precarious situation of all[2]. Shelter identifies one million people at risk of homelessness[3] and calculates the numbers homeless now as 307,000 (although admitting that this is a conservative estimate)[4]. In the London Borough of Newham one in twenty five people are homeless[5].

In his introduction Rob Ray rightly links the rise in rough sleeping, and homelessness in general, to the austerity policies pursued firstly by the coalition and then the Tory governments of Cameron and May. The present housing crisis however has deeper historical roots.

Post War
The Second World War resulted in a massive housing shortage. According to official estimates, enemy action destroyed 218,000 homes and further damaged 250,000 so as to make them uninhabitable, in comparison to

only around 190,000 houses completed during the war. Returning soldiers and their families took to squatting. An early victory resulted in local authorities being given the power to requisition unused dwellings for housing. Mass squatting began in August 1946, often organised by specific groups of ex-soldiers, the Communist Party and even the Labour Party, but the BBC also noted at the time a "strange new mood of orderly lawlessness" which had its own momentum as "once people realised that it could be done, it was done, all over the country"[6].

At the 1945 General Election, the Labour Party had boasted of its ability to solve the housing problem, and pledged to create a Ministry of Housing. Instead it handed the housing problem to Aneurin Bevan, to solve at the Ministry of Health[7]. Under attack over the housing crisis from both Conservative opposition and the right-wing media and in the face of widespread squatting Bevan, reluctantly, opted for the stopgap of prefabs. Many of the squatted military camps were handed over to the occupants and were eventually incorporated into wider public housing systems (being used as social housing well into the 1950s)[8]. Much the same would happen later with the squatting movement in the 1960s and 1970s and the rise of the housing associations. By the mid-1970s an estimated 20–30,000 people throughout Greater London had reclaimed, repaired and squatted thousands of empty dwellings earmarked for demolition[9]. Gradually many of these squats were licenced and, whilst many became housing co-ops, others were eventually taken over by housing associations and remain social housing today.

In the post-war period the two parties of government vied with each other to build more council homes. This reached a peak under the Conservative government of the 1950s, when the end of rationing and a growing economy meant that 250,000 new local authority homes a year were being erected. Much of the expansion was in the new towns designated by the previous Attlee government in land beyond the newly created green belt surrounding London – towns such as Hemel Hempstead, Harlow and Crawley. This boom continued in the 1960s, but increasingly quantity was at the expense of quality as "estates in the skies" and high rise blocks were constructed. One block, Ronan Point in east London, collapsed in 1968 following a gas explosion, killing four occupiers and injuring 17.

Alongside the boom in council house building there was an increase in owner-occupation, so the private rented sector shrank. By the end of the 1960s, Britain had as many owner-occupiers as renters. Broadly speaking the middle class were owner-occupiers; the working class council tenants.

House building of all kinds slowed following the oil crisis in 1973, which signalled the end of the mixed economy and 'full employment', the effect of which is still felt today. The capitalist crisis led to the election of the Thatcher government in 1979 and the era of neoliberalism. Thatcher took an idea initially proposed, but later disregarded, by Jim Callaghan: the sale of council homes to sitting tenants. Alongside this she vowed to end rent control and provided subsidies for mortgage payers, thus creating a bubble in house prices.

Right to Buy

Historically a small number of council houses had been sold to sitting tenants each year at a modest discount. At the 1979 general election, council-home sales featured prominently in the Conservative manifesto. In this slim pamphlet, the right to buy was given as much space as enormous issues such as education and health, and explained right down to the precise discounts to be offered to tenants. These were to start at 33% off their home's market value, and were to rise, according to how long they had rented it, to a maximum of 50% for tenants of 20 years' standing or longer. "We shall also ensure," promised the manifesto, "that

100% mortgages are available."[10] For any purchaser these were extremely generous terms.

In August 1980 Margaret Thatcher's first government published a Housing Act. Whilst it was long-winded and repetitive, there was a clear intention "to give ... the right to buy their homes ... to tenants of local authorities". It is important to remember that the government was by then barely a year old and already deeply unpopular.

Between October 1st 1980 and March 31st 2013 1,869,898 council houses and flats were sold under Right to Buy in England alone[11]. In 2015-17 there were 34,333 Right to Buy sales[12] in England.

In 1980 there were 6.5 million council dwellings in England, Scotland and Wales; that figure now stands at just over 2m, leading to the Independent to declare in one headline 'Council housing numbers hit lowest point since records began'[13].

Obviously many of these properties are no longer owned by the purchasers and a huge number are now rented to private tenants at market (i.e. unaffordable) rents. In 2016 the Communities and Local Government select committee announced that 40% of ex-council flats sold through right to buy were being rented out more expensively by private landlords[14]. As a result two neighbours can be paying vastly different rents in the same block of flats; with the private tenant paying up to four times the rent of the council tenant.

Whilst about half the proceeds of the sales were paid to the local authorities, the government required the money to be used to reduce their debt, rather than spending it on building replacement homes. In addition, local councils have been prevented from borrowing money to build more homes. At the 2018 Tory Party conference, Theresa May announced plans to scrap the council borrowing cap[15].

Rent Control

The introduction of rent control was a direct response to the rent strikes of 1915. In the midst of war, with most men fighting at the front, working class women were both working (particularly in munitions) and in charge of the home. Wages were officially frozen, unofficially they decreased[16]. Landlords tried to increase the rents (they do not have the moniker "greedy landlords" for nothing). The year before, in eight short weeks, rent-strikers in Leeds defeated a proposed rent rise of six pence. 1915 saw "Mary Barbour's Army" of women take action in Scotland.

Mary Barbour was born 1875 in Kilbarchan. She left school at 14, working initially as a wool twister and later a carpet printer, and married shipyard worker David at 21. Mary and her family settled in Govan in 1914, where she quickly joined the local Co-operative Guild and Independent Labour Party.

Mary formed a housing association with the women of South Govan in 1915. Along with other tenants' committees the direct aim was to prevent families from being evicted by all means, including physical action against Sheriffs' officers. Fellow rent-striker Helen Crawfurd recalled:.

"This is how they organised the resistance: one woman with a bell would sit in the tenement close, watching while the other women living in the tenement went on with their household duties. Whenever the Bailiff's Officer appeared to evict a tenant, the woman in the passage immediately rang the bell, and the other women put down whatever work they were doing and hurried to where the alarm was being raised.

"They would hurl flour bombs and other missiles at the bailiff, forcing him to make a hasty retreat. It is said they even pulled down his trousers to humiliate him![17]"

By November 1915, as many as 20,000 tenants were on rent strike, and the action was spreading beyond Glasgow to other parts of Scotland and south to England.

On November 17th the City cited 49 strikers for striking. Those prosecuted were mostly shipyard workers and their families. A wave of immediate sympathy walk-outs were called, and strikers assembled to march in a huge deputation to the Sheriff's court, with thousands of women among them. Lloyd George gave direct orders to release the tenants before matters escalated; the scene outside the court turned into a huge street party as the women and men celebrated their momentous victory[18].

Within a month the government had passed emergency legalisation making the victory complete[19]. That "temporary measure" was extended in 1919 and again in 1920, so by then 98% of housing was controlled by the Acts[20], due to the threat posed by returning soldiers who had the example of the Russian revolution and the simmering revolution in Germany. Although the number of properties subject to rent control fluctuated over the next 60 years, it covered most privately rented homes.

Initially Thatcher denied any plans to remove rent controls (whilst linking the cause of homelessness to rent control):

"Well now, just let me take two points. Do you know there are I think more boarded-up empty houses at the moment than there are homeless people? And there are more empty properties because people daren't rent them, because of the effect of some of the rent restriction Acts — they daren't rent them because of the difficulty of getting out a very unsatisfactory tenant. This is a thing that we must think about — there's no question of taking off rent control or fair rents or security of tenure, but there are a lot of empty properties boarded-up; there are a lot of empty flats because the landlord daren't let them."
— TV Interview for Thames TV *TV Eye* 12 April 1979[21]

Within a few months Michael Heseltine, then the Secretary of State for the Environment, introduced the Housing Act 1980 stating:

> "In recent years, in both the public and private sectors, one form of rent restraint or another has placed an intolerable financial burden on local authorities and private owners ... The public sector is following the course long familiar in the private sector, where increasing rent control over decades has forced owners to sell and not to let, or to allow properties to decay"[22].

The private sector was therefore going to come to the rescue and solve the housing crisis.

Although the Housing Act 1980 was largely a failure in this respect, as the procedures were too complex, the Tories succeeded in the Housing Act 1988. This created assured shorthold tenancies[23] and the later government of John Major simplified the procedure for landlords, making them the default option[24].

In doing so rent control was removed along with security of tenure and the dreaded Section 21 Notice was created. This means that no matter if you pay your rent in full and on time, that you are a model tenant in every way, the landlord can still evict you on a whim, provided they follow the correct legal procedure.

The shrinkage of the social housing sector and the corresponding growth of the private sector has left tenants in a precarious position, afraid to complain to landlords about the poor standards for fear of eviction. It has, in short, turned the clock back to the pre-second world war period.

Conditions in the private sector are extremely poor. A quarter of a million families in England are bringing up babies and young children in privately rented accommodation that failed to meet the "decent homes standard". To put that into context, one in five homes let at the top 20% of rents are non-decent, whilst one in three let at the bottom 20% of rents are non-decent[25].

A decent home is simply one that is free from any hazard that poses a serious threat to your health or safety, is in a reasonable state of repair, has reasonably modern facilities and has efficient heating and insulation. Not, you might think, too much to ask.

The reason conditions are so poor is profit. Landlords know that they can rent substandard homes and carrying out even basic repairs would reduce their profits. Meanwhile property prices continue to rise, even if they have slowed a bit, so the parasitic landlord cannot lose. Even landlords convicted of housing offences and judged unfit to be landlords continue to rent with impunity; the government created a rogue landlord database so that local councils could target the country's worst landlords, but, more than six months after the system started, not a single name had been added[26].

Subsidies

Whilst focusing tabloid attention on subsidies to council housing, Thatcher subsidised home ownership. Between 1979 and 1990, this subsidy rose from £2.5bn to more than £8bn, so that 9.7 million home owners benefited by the end of the 1990s.

This in turn led to a doubling of house prices over the decade, and laid the foundations for unsustainable levels of home ownership which contributed to the financial crash in 2008[27].

In fact, council housing has been making a profit since 2008, which has been paid to the Treasury. On April 1st 2012 all subsidies to existing council homes ceased and councils were forced to take on the additional debt. These costs have since been met from rents[28].

Pensions

Whether intentional or not, the removal of proper occupational pension provision during the Thatcher years encouraged many people to become landlords. The promise of continually increasing house prices, tax breaks (which have now ended) and the carrot that a tenant would pay your mortgage, leaving an asset to be sold on retirement, was too much to resist for many. As a result there are an estimated 2.5m landlords (based on data from HM Revenue and Customs) and 89% of UK landlords are private individuals[29]. They are therefore amateur landlords, not in the sense of not seeking a profit, but rather lacking the skills required to manage properties.

Given that about 5.3m people are renting privately, the average landlord owns just one or two properties. The Council of Mortgage Lenders in 2016 found that over 60% of landlords owned only a single rented property and almost half of all properties were purchased using a buy-to-let mortgage[30]. Whilst the recent tax changes may have prompted some landlords to sell up, there are still huge profits to be made. Estate agents Savills boasted that landlords "earned" £54bn in the year to June 2018[31].

Housing Associations

Although some of the traditional housing trusts, such as Peabody, were founded by religious philanthropists and date from the late 1800s, it is the period since 1974 that witnessed the significant growth and transformation of the housing association sector. 1979 saw the dawn of a neoliberal era in which housing associations came to take an increasingly central role in social housing provision. Housing associations benefited from state funding, as the Thatcher government diverted funds away from local councils and sought to expand the housing association sector by drawing in private finance to create "mixed funding" schemes.

Thus whilst council housebuilding ground to a halt, housing association housebuilding increased, although not at the same pace. More importantly the lines between public and private were deliberately blurred[32].

In 1988 the process started of the transfer of social housing from local authorities to housing associations. The 1997 Labour government made it clear that it would discourage local authorities from being landlords. In 2000 it required authorities with remaining housing stock to meet the new decent homes standard by 2010 and encouraged stock transfer as a way to achieve this[33]. Where this could not be achieved, due to tenant opposition (a ballot of tenants was required), arms-length management organisations were set up to take over the management of council housing. Between 1997 and 2010 almost a million council homes were transferred to housing associations, so 80% of all stock transfers took place under a Labour government.

Not content with stock transfers, councils, many Labour, began the process of demolishing estates and handing the land to housing associations or private developers, cheered on by Lord Adonis, a former Labour cabinet minister[34]. The most notorious of these was the Aylesbury, one of the largest council estates in Europe. Southwark council is demolishing the estate block by block. Before demolition, the Aylesbury estate had 2,402 homes being rented out by the council at social rents. A further 356 homes had been sold under right to buy and were in private ownership. The new development, to be built by the housing association Notting Hill Genesis, will have 1,323 units at social rent and 1,773 for private sale. A further 479 homes will be offered on a shared ownership basis[35]. This is therefore a net loss of 1,079 social housing homes.

Heygate, which was home for 3,000 Londoners, was demolished in 2014 after Southwark Council sold it for £50 million to Lendlease. The council spent almost the same amount forcing tenants out. In 2013, Southwark Council cut off heating and switched off the lifts, leaving tenants stranded. Ultimately just 82 of the new homes were social housing. Reportedly most of the other flats were sold abroad[36].

Elsewhere, resistance was more successful: plans for the largest sell off of council housing were defeated in Haringey and in Hammersmith and Fulham the Tory council's plans cost them the election. The BBC reported in September 2018 however that in London 118 sites are undergoing or facing regeneration, which will affect over 31,000 residents and nearly 8,000 homes could be lost over the next decade[37].

Demonstrating the tendency to monopoly inherent in capitalism, housing associations started a spate of mergers and take-overs which continues to this day[38]. The smaller diverse associations were swallowed by their larger rivals. Now they dwarf the largest of councils. Even Peabody was not immune, merging with Family Mosaic in 2017. A2Dominion has a housing stock of 34,000 and a turnover of £200m and Hyde Housing Association has a housing stock of 47,500 and a turnover of £243m[39]. L&Q has a housing stock of 70,000, whilst Clarion Housing Group has 125,000[40]. By way of contrast, the largest council housing authority, Birmingham, has a stock of 64,000 dwellings[41].

As housing associations were treated as big businesses so they began to act like them, renting homes for so-called affordable rents (in reality an unaffordable 80% of market rent), developing homes for sale rather than rent and getting rid of 'troublesome' tenants. Housing associations routinely use a mandatory ground for eviction against any tenant unfortunate enough to find themselves eight weeks or more in rent arrears[42]. In 2016/17, housing associations chief executives' average salary was £166,205, whilst Places for People saw fit to pay their Chief Executive £579,183 (including a bonus of £188,365), Clarion £376,199 and L&Q £344,000. The average wage of a housing officer meanwhile was £21,000, meaning many are entitled to Housing Benefit[43].

In 2017 housing associations made record profits of £3.5bn, not bad for a sector that is supposed to be charitable and not for profit[44]. Indeed it is difficult, if not impossible, to distinguish housing associations from any other property developing spivs.

Housing Benefit and Universal Credit
Much of the argument about housing subsidies has focused on Housing Benefit (now being replaced by Universal Credit Housing Costs). This is, of course, a very real subsidy, but it is a subsidy to greedy profiteering landlords rather than tenants. In 2015 Generation Rent showed that private landlords gained £26.7bn from UK taxpayers, a sum the equivalent of £1,000 for every single household in the country in a mixture of Housing benefit payments and tax relief[45]. Although some of that tax relief has now been ended, the Housing Benefit element alone was £9.3bn.

On April 7th 2008 the Labour government introduced the Local Housing Allowance (LHA) to calculate Housing Benefit entitlement for private sector tenants. Instead of an assessment of an individual property, levels were based on "Broad Rental Market Areas" and worse the level was set at the 30th percentile (i.e. the lowest third) for the region. In 2016 the rates were simply frozen, despite rents increasing. If your rent is above the LHA rate then you have to make up the shortfall.

In 2013 the Coalition government imposed the benefit cap as part of the austerity war on the poor. Whilst this led to a temporary fall in the Housing Benefit bill within two years it had overtaken the 2014 levels, as landlords continued to profit. Meanwhile between its 2013 rollout and November 2015, 69,900 households lost some housing benefit due to the cap[46], forcing those reliant on Housing Benefit further into poverty, giving families the stark choice of eating or paying the rent. As the government is forced to acknowledge, 49% of those affected by the benefit cap were lone parents with a youngest child under the age of five and of those almost half were working[47]. As the *New Statesman* put it: "In half of England, a family with two children living in a modest home must survive on £8 each a day". This would leave them at least £100 a week below the UK poverty line[48].

At the same time the government imposed the bedroom tax on social housing tenants. On average, a tenant affected by the bedroom tax is losing between £14 and £25 a week for what the government argued were spare rooms. Heaven forbid that council and housing association tenants should have a little extra space in the rabbit hutches built in the '70s, '80s and '90s. At the time, the architect of the government's war on the poor, Iain Duncan Smith, lived rent free in a £2m country home with at least four spare bedrooms[49]. Evaluating the policy in December 2015, the government unsurprisingly found that three-quarters of those affected by the bedroom tax said they'd had to cut back on food. The same research found that 46% said they had cut back on heating and 33% on travel[50]. Even the United Nations' special investigator on housing, Raquel Rolnik, argued that the policy should be scrapped[51].

The third plank of the government's war against the poor is the introduction of Universal Credit, a system of benefit cuts and built in delays. Everywhere it is introduced it brings heightened risk of hunger, debt and rent arrears, ill-health and homelessness. On the housing front, as well as being subject to the same benefit caps as Housing Benefit, Universal Credit is paid monthly in arrears. That means a minimum of five weeks after you claim before you get paid. That is, of course, before any other delay in processing the claim.

The roll out of Universal Credit has been subject to numerous delays, the most recent being announced on October 16th 2018[52], but this does not of course help those already in the nightmare system. Most people would be hard pressed to come up with a better strategy for increasing homelessness and rough sleeping than Universal Credit.

Work makes you Poor and Homeless

Theresa May continues to trot out the mantra that working hard is "the best route out of poverty", most recently in a riposte to the Archbishop of Canterbury (after he criticised the government's record in tackling poverty)[53]. The reality however is that work makes you poor and homeless.

A study by Cardiff University found that 60% of Britons in poverty are in working families. The study found in-work poverty was disproportionately concentrated in households in private rented housing, who have been hit by a combination of rising rents and caps on housing benefit. As they point out, if this form of housing tenure grows as projected there will be a corresponding increase in numbers facing in-work poverty[54].

In one emergency night shelter in the centre of London about one third of those seeking a bed are working. As Aditya Chakrabortty noted in the *Guardian*, it was a roll call of Britain's consumer economy: Starbucks, Eat, Pret, pubs, McDonald's, a courier for Deliveroo[55].

The Local Government Ombudsman, Michael King, warns that homelessness is now a serious risk for working families with stable jobs who cannot find somewhere affordable to live after being evicted by private-sector landlords seeking higher rents. King said that nurses, taxi drivers, hospitality staff and council workers were among those assisted by his office after being made homeless and placed in often squalid and unsafe temporary accommodation by local authorities[56].

Labour and the Benefit System

The Labour Party has pledged to scrap the sanctions regime and the Bedroom Tax, reinstate Housing Benefit for under-21s and scrap cuts to Bereavement Support Payment. In addition Labour will reform and redesign Universal Credit, ending six-week delays in payment and the "rape clause"[57].

Assuming that Labour get elected with a majority and assuming they stick to these pledges (two big "ifs"), this will remove some of the Tories attacks on the poor. What will be left untouched is the uncaring and remote bureaucracy which, as Andrew describes, is so difficult to navigate.

Nor will this address the refusal of the majority of landlords to accept tenants in receipt of benefits. Andrew questions why such discrimination is allowed to continue, but it remains rife throughout the private sector. Universal Credit it simply making matter worse: In November 2017 a private landlord, GAP Property, sent Section 21 Notices to every single one of its 350 tenants, not due to them being in rent arrears, but due to many being switched to Universal Credit[58]. This is not however a new phenomenon. In 2014 one notorious Kent landlord, Fergus Wilson, sought to evict 200 tenants just for being on housing benefit[59]. This may however amount to unlawful discrimination on one or more of the grounds in the Equality Act 2010[60]. In February 2018 the BBC reported that one tenant, Rosie Keogh, won compensation for sex discrimination from letting agent Nicholas George in Birmingham in a case that was settled out of court[61].

Rents

Historically it was considered that spending 30% of income on housing was a reasonable amount, regardless of whether you lived in the UK, USA or Europe. By 2017 when the average private rent in London stood at £1,590 per calendar month, on average tenants were spending 41.1% of their annual salaries on rent in 2017. Whilst this was the average, one in seven tenants privately renting from a landlord was paying more than half of their income in rent[62].

Not surprisingly this is simply unaffordable. Indeed Shelter estimate that rents in over half of England are unaffordable. As a result 38% of families with children who are renting privately have cut down on buying food to pay their rent[63]. Nor is this the preserve of the young. The National Housing Federation reported that 44% of private renters over the age of 50 – at least half a million people – are forced to make drastic decisions to cover the cost of their rent. This includes borrowing money from their own children, taking out loans and not buying food[64].

And as the Chartered Institute of Housing (CIH) warned:

"LHA rates are now so seriously out of line with local rents that private renting has become unaffordable for most low income tenants and this substantially increases their risk of homelessness. The longer the freeze continues, the wider the gap becomes and the more costly it becomes to restore LHA rates to their full value."[65]

Ending Rough Sleeping
The government meanwhile pledged (in March 2018) to end rough sleeping by 2027. Rob in his Introduction comments on the litany of previous broken commitments. But if we take this one at face value for the moment, what the government is saying is that for the next nine years rough sleeping will continue. So far entrenched is the homelessness crisis, so far has rough sleeping become the norm, that politicians are content to state publicly that it will continue in the medium term future.

None of this is new of course. Sir George Young, then the government Chief Whip (and previously a prominent member of the Housing Commission on Westminster Council) said in the 1980s: "The homeless? Aren't they the people you step over when you are coming out of the opera?"

Regardless of government statements, all neutral observers expect homelessness to rise not fall over the next decade.

Violence and Death

Andrew depressingly details the violence faced by rough sleepers, the casual assaults, the robbery of meagre possessions, the rape of women, the destruction of belongings by the police, the use of alarms to keep people awake.

Crisis found that:

- More than one in three have been deliberately been hit, kicked, or experienced some other form of violence while homeless.
- Over one in three (34%) have had things thrown at them.
- Almost one in 10 (9%) have been urinated on while homeless.
- More than one in 20 (7%) have been the victim of a sexual assault.
- Almost half (48%) have been intimidated or threatened with violence whilst homeless.
- Six in 10 (59%) have been verbally abused or harassed[66].

As George Orwell once discovered: "It is fatal to look hungry. It makes people want to kick you."[67]

The Vagrancy Act 1824, gives police the powers to arrest and detain for up to three months anyone found, "lodging in any barn or outhouse, or in any deserted or unoccupied building, or in the open air, or under a tent, or in any cart or waggon, not having any visible means of subsistence"[68]. In 2016/17, a Freedom of Information request reported 1,810 prosecutions under the Act, and as recently as 2015 the number was more than 3,000.

Public Spaces Protection Orders (PSPOs)[69] allow local authorities to enforce on-the-spot fines for certain activities. Predictably, local authorities are applying these powers to target homeless people by sanctioning what they do in public spaces: street drinking, begging, camping in parks, defecating and urinating and in some cases even sleeping[70]. Soup kitchens have also been targeted by Councils such as Westminster and Manchester.

Criminal Behaviour Orders (CBOs) introduced in 2014 give courts powers including banning people from areas or from drinking in public. Homeless Link said CBOs prevented homeless people from accessing vital services.

The leader of Windsor Council called for removal of the homeless before the royal wedding on May 19th 2018 and people sleeping rough near Windsor Castle had their sleeping bags and other possessions removed in the week leading up to the wedding[71]. One in 10 councils abuse their powers to criminalise rough sleepers.

As the Chief Executive of Crisis, Jon Sparkes, said:

> "In fact, homeless people are far more likely to be victims of crime than perpetrators, and rough sleepers are 17 times more likely to be victims of violence compared to the general public. They deserve better than to be treated as criminals simply because they have nowhere to live"[72].

Other tactics include physical deterrents (sometimes referred to as "defensive architecture"), noise deterrents and wetting down. Spikes were installed at Pall Mall Court, Manchester and in Curtain Road in Shoreditch London, where locals responded by placing mattresses over them[73]. Andrew details his battle with Marks and Spencer over the use of noise. Wetting down is used routinely by Westminster City Council, where the streets are hosed down in the middle of the might. Major transport systems have regular warnings about giving to "professional beggars", deterring people from even this simple act of kindness.

Then there is the charitable collusion with immigration officials exposed by *Corporate Watch*.

More depressingly still, the *Guardian* research showed that the number of homeless people recorded dying on streets or in temporary accommodation has more than doubled over the last five years, to an average of more than one death a week in 2017. The average age of a rough sleeper at death was 43, nearly half the UK life expectancy[74]. Since 2017 the rate of death has increased to three per week on average, according to the Bureau of Investigative Journalism, which is attempting to collect their stories[75].

Friedrich Engels once coined a phrase for the ruling class placing "hundreds of proletarians in such a position that they inevitably meet a too early and an unnatural death": Social murder[76]. This is different to murder and manslaughter, as no individual can be blamed; social murder is explicitly committed by the capitalist class against the poorest in society. The homeless are just among the most recent victims.

Homelessness Legislation

All this must be set against the backdrop of some of the most robust homelessness legalisation in Europe. Part 7 of the Housing Act 1996, even before the recent Homelessness Reduction Act amendments, requires local councils to house homeless people who are eligible (a kind of immigration test), in priority need (those who are pregnant, with children or otherwise vulnerable) and not intentionally homeless (a punitive blame mechanism). Andrew explains the practical difficulties of accessing such help, even if you qualify.

The reality however is that those who are accepted as homeless by councils are housed in modern day slums. Connect House is a former office block in Mitcham, bought by its current owners for January 2015 for £3,100,000. Some 200 children, and their families, have been placed at Connect House by one of four local authorities. The property is managed by Easy Lettings and licensed by Merton Council, and three other councils, for temporary housing. It contains 84 flats[77]. If we assume an average rent of £35 per night, then that is rent of over £1m per year, so the cost of buying the building will be recovered in just three years.

Property investors talk about the yield, a way of measuring the profitability of investing. A good yield is said to be 8-10%. The yield for Connect House is 34%. The biggest profits are to be made out of the poorest.

Over the past three years, local councils have spent over £2.6bn on temporary housing[78], all of which comes from council tax payers and goes into the pockets of private landlords. English councils spent over £937m on temporary accommodation for homeless households in the financial year ending April 2017 alone[79].

Good-quality, sustainable social housing can be built for around £100,000 per unit in upfront costs. Therefore the annual spend on temporary accommodation would build 9,370 new homes in England every year.

Needless to say the conditions in temporary accommodation are very poor. A lack of locks on doors, hostile or greedy landlords, overcrowding, and contact with people misusing substances when others are trying to quit [80]. Curfews, the inability to have guests, no access to a kitchen[81], infestations, damp and Dickensian conditions are rife.

The number of households living in temporary accommodation has risen to more than 79,000 in England. Over 120,000 children are homeless[82]. In 2017, 55% of families living in temporary accommodation were working. This represents over 33,000 families who were trying to hold down a job despite having nowhere stable to live[83].

Councils seek to export their homelessness. 1,200 households were moved out of London in the first half of 2018, the highest level in six years. Birmingham placed almost 2,000 households outside the City. As a result people are forced to quit their jobs, give up their education and travel for hours to visit family and friends.

Even the term 'temporary' is a misnomer designed to cover up the extent of the crises and misery. One in ten households have been in temporary accommodation for more than five years and for some families in the London boroughs of Harrow and Camden the period is as long as 19 years[84]. One person had spent 36 years in "temporary" accommodation![85]

In April 2018 the homelessness provisions were extended by the Homelessness Reduction Act. In theory the gainers should be the single homeless, who are now supposed to be offered meaningful help in relieving their homelessness, but this assistance stops short of any actual housing having to be provided. It is too early to be certain what, if any, impact these changes have had, but in practice most single homeless people, certainly most rough sleepers, are likely to be directed to the kind of direct access hostels that made Andrew feel so afraid. Given the options, it is unsurprising that many people opt for the streets.

Empty Homes and Social Housing
The obvious answer to the housing crisis is to build more homes, particularly social housing, a point Andrew makes in his diary. There are however huge numbers of empty dwellings and the number is increasing.

Official government data shows that the number of empty homes in England in October 2017 was 605,891 and that 205,293 were classed as long-term empty properties (empty for longer than six months). Therefore there are sufficient empty homes to immediately house all the rough sleepers and about two-thirds of those who are homeless[86].

That figure of 205,293 is certainly an underestimate. As Action on Empty Homes notes, derelict properties are not classed as dwellings for Council Tax purposes (the main source of data) and an owner may not inform the local authority that their property is empty, leading to undercounting. The point is made that owners who are still liable for Council Tax payments may have no reason to let their local authority know that the property is vacant. The data does not include dwellings where there is an exemption from paying Council Tax. So, for example, it does not include unoccupied clergy dwellings or properties held in the possession of a mortgage lender or trustee in a bankruptcy[87]. Research by the Liberal Democrats put the figure at 216,000 (and that more than 11,000 homes across the UK have been empty for 10 years or more)[88].

Nor is it the case that these properties are in the wrong locations. In London there are 20,237 long-term empty properties and in the North West (which includes Manchester) 39,344. It is important to stress that the figures on long-term empty properties relate to residential properties only, not empty office blocks.

Action on Empty Homes argues that there is a variety of reasons why properties are long-term empty (personal and financial circumstances of the property owners, inheriting a property, the new owner may take some time to decide what to do, or to sort out the property before it is put on the market for rent or sale, a property may require substantial repairs before it can be re-let, but the landlord is putting off doing this work, often related to time or money constraints, people or companies have bought properties to redevelop). However, it is clear that in central locations, particularly London, but also other cities, properties are bought by wealthy speculators who snap up homes as investments and leave them empty while waiting for the value to increase before selling them on.

Not all the empty properties are in the private sector. Some are social housing, although that figure has been steadily falling (not least because empty dwellings are often auctioned off) but some are owned by central government. In May 2003 the Labour government noted that although government-owned housing stock comprises only a small proportion of the total, the proportion vacant was "considerably higher" than the national average, running at about 10%[89]. The bulk of government-owned housing belongs to agencies or trusts of four departments – the Ministry of Defence[90], Department for Transport, Department of Health and the

Home Office. Some of these have subsequently been sold, but figures are now hard to come by because, as Lord Bridges of Headley, Parliamentary Secretary for the Cabinet Office, revealed in June 2015 information on the number of vacant houses and flats owned by departments or their agencies is not held centrally[91].

Southwark has the largest number of empty homes of any London borough, a staggering 5,418, as of November 2017, with 1,035 empty for more than two years. Prior to the last local elections the project Who Owns England tried to discover what these homes were. The majority empty for more than six months were privately owned, although there were large numbers of council properties particularly on the Aylesbury Estate. The majority of empty dwellings were of lower value, falling into Council Tax bands A-C, although there were also "luxury" flats (for example all 10 of the penthouse flats in the upper floors of the Shard remained unsold, five years after being marketed, perhaps not surprising as they were asking £30m or more)[92].

Local councils do have a range of powers and incentives to bring empty homes back into use. These include Empty Dwelling Management Orders, Council Tax exemptions and premiums, enforced sales, compulsory purchase, and measures to secure the improvement of empty properties.

The main power is Empty Dwelling Management Orders (EDMOs). The Liberal Democrat research showed that only one in 13 councils is making use of EDMOs (although during the same period councils did return 23,000 empty homes back into use) and just 19 of the 247 councils in England and Wales that responded had used an EDMO in the past five years. Previously a council could make a EDMO after a property had been empty for six months. The Coalition government (which, of course, included the Lib Dems) restricted the use of EDMOs. The empty property must be a nuisance, a property has to stand empty for at least two years and the property owner has to be given at least three months' notice before the order can be issued[93]. This was done in the name of "protecting civil liberties".

There have been stacks of reports (official, semi-official and critical of governments) over the past 30 years which have identified the failure to build council homes as a (if not the) key factor in the housing crisis, none of which have made any real difference. There are a number of reasons why councils do not build homes for rented social housing. High land values act as a significant problem, there is the fear of Right to Buy being used, meaning that the investment is lost, and the inability of local authorities to borrow money for this purpose. There is also a backlog of repairs, with more than half a million social homes in England failing to meet the decent homes standard[94].

Then there is the political opposition. Many council tenants have been treated with distain, their complaints and concerns dismissed. They are either reviled as scroungers or not in need of council housing at all. The Tory government sought to end "lifetime" tenancies in 2015[95] (after all who needs a home for their entire life?) and anyone not aspiring to home ownership is treated with suspicion. Whilst there was a time when council housing was part of the welfare state – something that was there for anyone, of whatever class, who wanted it – now along with the rest of the welfare state it must be dismantled. This, in turn, means vilifying the occupiers.

Whilst council tenants have long been aware of this, the callous disregard for safety was revealed by Grenfell. All the warnings of the tenants, all the attempts to get answers about the refurbishment of the block, were simply ignored with a devastating outcome. It would, however, be naive to think that even the death of 72 people will lead to change; the fire in which six people died in July 2009 at the 12-storey Lakanal House in Camberwell changed nothing.

The Tories will not build social housing. Even in lifting the cap on what councils can borrow to build homes, May said:

"Solving the housing crisis is the biggest domestic policy challenge of our generation. We cannot make the case for capitalism if ordinary working people have no chance of owning capital."[96]

Thus neatly linking the building of council homes to home ownership. In reality the Tories will press for (un)affordable rents, part buy part rent and homes for sale, rather than social housing.

Labour has pledged to build one million new genuinely affordable homes over 10 years. In addition they propose to redefine "affordable housing" as linked to local income and scrap the "affordable rent", suspend (but not end) the Right to Buy, provide new funding powers for councils and housing associations and transform the planning system with a new duty to deliver affordable homes, an English Sovereign Land Trust to make more land available more cheaply and an end to the "viability" loophole that lets developers dodge their contribution to more affordable homes[97]. Whether they will deliver on these promises remains to be seen, but building a million homes over a 10-year period will not solve the housing crisis.

Whilst the restriction on council borrowing has been removed, high land values continue to be a huge barrier to building social housing. No politician is going to suggest that land should be devalued; that would mean house prices falling and the money that home owners have "made" disappearing (even if the profit is largely paper-based, realisable only by downsizing or on death). For some homeowners it would mean negative equity. It is also an issue beyond political control; if the house price bubble bursts like it did in 2008/9 the government will be reduced to a mere spectator. Then house prices fell by an average of 15.9%, but in some areas fell by 50%[98]. Whilst it would take a huge crash to make properties affordable, it is not inconceivable.

Private Property

The private sector has been an abject failure in providing housing. The state sector, despite the problems of reducing standards, poor design and lack of repairs, was better, but the state only responds when it perceives the interest of capital to be threatened: as It did in response to a rent strike or mass squatting for example. A change of government is not enough.

Ultimately the housing crisis will not be solved whilst private property persists. Instead of being a commodity, to be traded for its exchange value, land needs to be "a common treasury for all"[99]. We need to radically change the way we live, use land and occupy housing. This is impossible within the constraints of the present system. As Engels put it:

> "It is not that the solution of the housing question simultaneously solves the social question, but that only by the solution of the social question, that is, by the abolition of the capitalist mode of production, is the solution of the housing question made possible."[100]

In the absence of revolutionary change, resistance will continue. Interspaced throughout Andrew's diary are examples of resistance taken from Freedom and other sources. Many other examples could be cited, from the occupation of a number of empty homes on the Aylesbury Estate, the New Era estate, Focus E15, Sweets Way Resists, Stop the Haringey Development and the London Coalition Against Poverty direct action casework to name but a few. For the moment we have to celebrate small victories, such as getting Marks and Spencer to turn off the night-time alarm.

— Tony Martin

NOTES

1. https://www.homeless.org.uk/ sites/default/files/site-attachments/ Homeless%20Link%20-%20 analysis%20of%20rough%20 sleeping%20statistics%20for%20 England%202017.pdf

2. Shelter: http://media.shelter.org.uk/ home/press_releases/8_million_ people_one_pay_check_away_from_ being_unable_to_pay_for_their_home

3. https://england.shelter.org.uk/__data/ assets/pdf_file/0005/1391675/LHA_ analysis_note_FINAL.pdf

4. https://england.shelter.org.uk/__data/ assets/pdf_file/0017/1440053/8112017_ Far_From_Alone.pdf

5. Ibid

6. https://squattinglondon.wordpress. com/2017/07/18/the-1946-squatters/

7. How Labour governed, 1945-1951, Libcom.org

8. https://squattinglondon.wordpress. com/2017/07/18/the-1946-squatters/

9. Sisterhood and Squatting in the 1970s: Feminism, Housing and Urban Change in Hackney , Christine WallHistory Workshop Journal, Volume 83, Issue 1, 1 April 2017

10. The Right to Buy, Alan Murie

11. https://www.gov.uk/ Government/statistical-data-sets/ live-tables-on-social-housing-sales

12. https://assets.publishing.service.gov. uk/Government/uploads/system/ uploads/attachment_data/file/661544/ Social_Housing_Sales_2016-17.pdf

13. https://www.independent.co.uk/news/ uk/politics/council-housing-uk-lowest- level-records-began-a8059371.html

14. https://www.parliament.uk/business/ committees/committees-a-z/ commons-select/communities- and-local-Government-committee/ news-parliament-2015/ right-to-buy-report-published-15-16/

15. https://www.insidehousing.co.uk/ home/home/theresa-may-announces- plan-to-scrap-council-borrowing- cap-58468

16. Women's Wages in Britain and Australia During the First World War, Jennifer Crew, Labour History No. 57 (Nov., 1989.

17. Remember Mary Barbour C. Burness, Scottish Labour History

18. 1915: Glasgow Rent Strike, Libcom and Rent Strikes: People's Struggle for Housing in West Scotland, 1890-1916 Joseph Melling

19. Increase of Rent and Mortgage Interest (War Restrictions) Act 1915

20. The History of the Law of Landlord and Tenant in England and Wales, Mark Wonnacott, 2011

21. https://www.margaretthatcher.org/ document/104040

22. https://api.parliament.uk/historic-hansard/commons/1980/jan/15/housing-bill

23. See Chapter 2 Housing Act 1988

24. Housing Act 1988, as amended by the Housing Act 1996

25. https://www.york.ac.uk/news-and-events/news/2018/research/housing-review-rugg/

26. https://www.theguardian.com/business/2018/oct/23/Governments-rogue-landlord-list-empty-after-six-months

27. https://www.theguardian.com/housing-network/2012/jan/27/Government-subsidised-social-housing-rent

28. See Chartered Institute of Housing's UK Housing Review annually.

29. https://www.paragonbank.co.uk/helpful-information/news-and-media/mortgage-blogs/2017-year-in-review-The-buy-to-let-market

30. CML Research, The profile of UK private landlords, December 2016

31. https://www.thetimes.co.uk/edition/business/bonanza-for-landlords-as-more-british-people-rent-homes-frdvh7z89

32. Facilitated by the Housing Act 1988

33. https://www.jrf.org.uk/report/evolution-stock-transfer-housing-associations

34. https://www.ft.com/content/4129abaa-cf16-11e4-893d-00144feab7de

35. https://www.theguardian.com/cities/2018/sep/12/london-council-aylesbury-estate-development-southwark-financial-riskhttp://35percent.org/the-southwark-clearances/

36. https://www.vice.com/en_uk/article/qkq4bx/every-flat-in-a-new-south-london-development-has-been-sold-to-foreign-investors

37. https://www.bbc.co.uk/news/uk-england-london-45196994

38. In April 2018 Notting Hill Housing and Genesis Housing Association amalgamated to form Notting Hill Genesis, one of the largest HA's.

39. https://www.theguardian.com/housing-network/2012/jun/08/housing-association-profiles

40. http://g15london.org.uk/

41. https://data.birmingham.gov.uk/dataset/social-housing-stock

42. Ground 8 of Schedule 2, Housing Act 1988.

43. https://www.insidehousing.co.uk/insight/insight/chief-executive-salary-survey-2017-52551

44. https://www.theguardian.com/housing-network/2018/feb/28/housing-associations-record-profits-affordable-homes

45. http://www.generationrent.org/making_money_like_a_landlord

46. House of Commons Research Paper, The Benefit Cap, No 06294, 21 November 2016

47. https://assets.publishing.service.gov.uk/Government/uploads/system/uploads/attachment_data/file/624758/Estimated-impact-of-the-benefit-cap-on-parents.pdf

48. https://www.newstatesman.com/politics/economy/2017/03/benefit-cap-may-be-popular-it-plunging-private-renters-poverty

49. It would be impolite to mention the swimming pool and tennis courts: https://www.mirror.co.uk/news/uk-news/bedroom-tax-iain-duncan-smith-1794517

50. https://assets.publishing.service.gov.uk/Government/uploads/system/uploads/attachment_data/file/506407/rsrs-evaluation.pdf

51. https://www.theguardian.com/society/2013/sep/11/bedroom-tax-should-be-axed-says-un-investigator It should be noted that in Scotland the Scottish Government has ensured that no social housing tenants are left out of pocket by the Bedroom Tax.

52. https://www.bbc.co.uk/news/uk-45870553

53. https://www.telegraph.co.uk/politics/2018/09/26/theresa-may-hits-back-archbishop-canterbury-saying-work-best/

54. https://www.cardiff.ac.uk/news/view/758111-record-levels-of-in-work-poverty-revealed

55. https://www.theguardian.com/commentisfree/2016/dec/20/working-homeless-britain-economy-minimum-wage-zero-hours?CMP=fb_gu

56. https://www.lgo.org.uk/information-centre/news/2017/dec/changing-face-of-homelessness-highlighted-in-ombudsman-report

57. https://labour.org.uk/manifesto/social-security/

58. https://www.propertyindustryeye.com/letting-agents-shocking-notices-to-quit-to-all-its-tenants-raised-by-corbyn-in-prime-ministers-questions/

59. https://www.bbc.co.uk/news/av/uk-25631605/kent-landlord-evicts-200-housing-benefit-tenants

60. It is against the law to discriminate against anyone on grounds of their: age; being or becoming a transsexual person; being married or in a civil partnership; being pregnant or on maternity leave; disability; race including colour, nationality, ethnic or national origin; religion, belief or lack of religion/belief; sex; sexual orientation.

61. https://www.bbc.co.uk/news/education-42979242

62. https://www.statista.com/statistics/752217/household-rent-to-income-ratio-by-region-uk/

63. http://media.shelter.org.uk/home/press_releases/rents_in_over_half_of_england_are_unaffordable,_new_research_shows

64. https://www.housing.org.uk/resource-library/browse/experiences-of-those-aged-50-in-the-private-rented-sector/

65. http://www.cih.org/resources/PDF/Policy%20free%20download%20pdfs/Missing%20the%20target%20final.pdf

66. https://www.crisis.org.uk/about-us/media-centre/crisis-reveals-scale-of-violence-and-abuse-against-rough-sleepers-as-charity-opens-its-doors-for-christmas/

67. Down and Out in Paris and London, George Orwell

68. Sections 3 of the Vagrancy Act 1824; House of Commons Research Paper, Rough Sleepers and Anti-Social Behaviour (England), No 07836, 27 February 2018

69. Section 59 Anti-social Behaviour, Crime and Policing Act 2014

70. http://theconversation.com/britains-dark-history-of-criminalising-homeless-people-in-public-spaces-74097https://www.independent.co.uk/news/uk/politics/britain-s-dark-history-of-criminalising-homeless-people-in-public-spaces-a7626531.html

71. https://www.theguardian.com/society/2018/jan/03/windsor-council-calls-removal-homeless-people-before-royal-wedding; https://inews.co.uk/news/homeless-near-windsor-have-belongings-removed-royal-wedding-sleeping-bags/

72. House of Commons Research Paper, Rough Sleepers and Anti-Social Behaviour (England), No 07836, 27 February 2018

73. http://betterthanspikes.tumblr.com/

74. https://www.theguardian.com/society/2018/apr/11/deaths-of-uk-homeless-people-more-than-double-in-five-years

75. https://www.thebureauinvestigates.com/stories/2018-04-23/dying-homeless

76. The Condition of the Working-Class in England, Friedrich Engels

77. https://mitchamhistorynotes.wordpress.com/2017/11/11/connect-house/ https://www.bbc.co.uk/news/education-41776369

78. https://www.huffingtonpost.co.uk/entry/david-lammy-dickensian_uk_5a01de30e4b066c2c03a73d7

79. https://www.insidehousing.co.uk/insight/insight/the-cost-of-homelessness-council-spend-on-temporary-accommodation-revealed-57720

80. https://www.ippr.org/files/publications/pdf/not-home_Dec2014.pdf

81. https://www.scottishhousingnews.com/24202/impact-of-living-in-temporary-accommodation-laid-bare-in-new-report/

82. https://assets.publishing.service.gov.uk/Government/uploads/system/uploads/attachment_data/file/721285/Statutory_Homelessness_and_Prevention_and_Relief_Statistical_Release_Jan_to_Mar_2018_-_REVISED.pdf

83. https://england.shelter.org.uk/__data/assets/pdf_file/0004/1545412/2018_07_19_Working_Homelessness_Briefing.pdf

84. https://www.huffingtonpost.co.uk/entry/david-lammy-dickensian_uk_5a01de30e4b066c2c03a73d7

85. https://www.ippr.org/files/publications/pdf/not-home_Dec2014.pdf

86. House of Commons Research Paper, Empty Homes (England), No 3012, 13 June 2018

87. http://www.actiononemptyhomes.org/wp-content/uploads/2018/03/final_ehe_2018_web.pdf

88. https://www.bbc.co.uk/news/uk-42536418

89. http://webarchive.nationalarchives.gov.uk/20120920011759/http://www.communities.gov.uk/documents/housing/pdf/138826.pdf

90. The MoD faces their own self-imposed housing crisis brought about by the use of sale and leaseback schemes.

91. https://www.parliament.uk/written-questions-answers-statements/written-question/lords/2015-06-02/HL217

92. https://whoownsengland.org/2018/04/20/why-are-there-over-5400-empty-homes-in-southwark/

93. The Housing (Empty Dwelling Management Orders) (Prescribed Period of Time and Additional Prescribed Requirements) (England) (Amendment) Order 2012: 2625

94. https://www.independent.co.uk/news/uk/home-news/uk-social-housing-health-and-safety-standards-failures-england-a7845961.html

95. Through the introduction of so-called flexible tenancies, although councils do not have to use them

96. https://www.telegraph.co.uk/politics/2018/10/03/theresa-mays-conservative-party-conference-speech-full-transcript/

97. https://labour.org.uk/issues/housing-for-the-many/

98. http://news.bbc.co.uk/1/hi/business/7812108.stm; https://www.theguardian.com/money/2008/nov/22/property-crash-uk-house-prices

99. https://libcom.org/history/1642-1652-diggers-levellers

100. Frederick Engels, The Housing Question, 1887

ABOUT THE CONTRIBUTORS

Andrew Fraser was brought up in Gateshead, Tyneside in the 1970s and began his journalistic career as a reporter for the *Stockport Express Advertiser* before moving into celebrity magazine writing. Fetching up at *OK!* magazine in the noughties, he covered the bizarre sleb scene of Kerry Katona, Jordan and Jade Goody, eventually being promoted to chief writer. He has interviewed stars from Chaka Khan, Joan Collins and Lionel Richie to Gazza, Lindsay Lohan and Amy Winehouse — one of the last she ever gave. Fraser's previous book, a travelogue called *Tripping The Flight Fantastic*, was published in 2016 by Bradt and he continues to blog at facebook.com/diaryofaroughsleeper. We considered outlining the events which led to him becoming homeless in East London, but felt that it is his story now which is of importance.

Freedom Press and its media arm Freedom News (freedomnews.org.uk) is the oldest anarchist publishing house in the English-speaking world. Founded in 1886, the press has a supremely rich political history and continues to publish a journal which first won notoriety through its defence of the Chicago Haymarket Martyrs during the fight for the eight-hour work day. Based in Whitechapel since 1968, many of the most important anarchist thinkers of the 19th and 20th centuries have written in its pages. *A Beautiful Idea: History of the Freedom Press Anarchists*, was published in October 2018 and a catalogue of its many books can be found via its online shop at freedompress.org.uk.

Rob Ray is a former newspaper editor and current publishing co-ordinator at Freedom Press. He has edited a number of titles brought out by the Press in recent years and is the author of *A Beautiful Idea*.

George F Has spent many years in squatting scenes all over Britain and Europe. He is a writer, performance poet and farmer who has travelled working with socially excluded groups from the homeless in London to street kids in Kuala Lumpur. He published his first book *Total Shambles*, a personal memoir of political squatting in London, in 2015.

Tony Martin Is a lawyer and activist specialising in housing and homelessness.

Corporate Watch (corporatewatch.org) is a not-for-profit co-operative providing critical information on the social and environmental impacts of corporations and capitalism. Since 1996 its research, journalism, analysis and training has supported people affected by corporations and those taking action for radical social change. It has published numerous books including *Investigating Companies: A Do It Yourself Handbook* and *Struggles for Autonomy in Kurdistan*. In 2018 the group released *Prison Island* and *The UK Border Regime*.

Squatters of London Action Paper (S.L.A.P.) is an irregular freesheet published in London since January 2016 by political squatters in the city. Stylistically punk, it aims to help connect the city's self-organised homeless in some of London's vast array of empty properties.

Manchester Activist Network was a shortlived but successful group which organised with the city's rough sleeping population in the 2016-18 period. Along with Lousy Badger Media and art collective Loose Space it helped self-organised people occupy multiple large sites across the city and pushed rough sleeping up the council agenda.